HELTER SKELTER...

Culturea

Copyright © 2024 by Culturea
All rights reserved.

Text and cover : © Culturea
Copyright © 2024 by *Culturea* a branch of *Les Prairies numériques* (Hérault, 34)
Find our catalog at http://culturea.fr/
Contact: infos@culturea.fr
Distribution : Ingram
Typographic design and layout: Derek Murphy, USA
Cover design : Canva
ISBN: 9791041989997

Legal deposit: March 2024

No part of this publication may be reproduced, distributed, or transmitted in any form
or by any means, including photocopying, recording, or other electronic or mechanical methods,
without the prior written permission of the publisher, except as permitted
by U.S. copyright law.

For permission requests, contact infos@culturea.fr

This book supports *Plantons Pour l'Avenir*, an endowment fund for the reforestation of French
forests with more than 400 forest reforestation projects supported since 2014 across France.
https://www.plantonspourlavenir.fr/

Frederic Monneyron

HELTER SKELTER…

A novel

1.

Damn it. The temperature already was above 80° F, at 10.30 in the morning. It would prove impossible to remain dressed as she was. She would not stand her stockings. Possibly, when she took them out of her drawer, she thought being in her native California, for just one moment. But, here in Sarasota at the beginning of May, it was warm, and very humid. She opened the sliding window, walked a few steps by the pool sparkling in the sunshine. No, "Muggy. Definitely muggy" she told herself. For sure, the car and then the airport terminal would be air-conditioned. But at noon, the heat would still rise.

    She came back into the house, and watched through the windowpanes, beyond the thick Kikuyu lawn, a neighbor's yacht slowly sailing to the Gulf of Mexico on the Waterway. All this water. The very definition of Florida. Florida, an improbable conjugation of the United States, its dreams and tensions. It may be why she settled down there some years ago; when her modeling career had come to an end, she preferred mosquitoes and alligators to returning on the Pacific Coast. She thought of Marc.

Back in her bedroom, she sat in front of her dressing table, fixed her make-up, a light blush and a dark-red lipstick, kicked her pumps off and had her stockings slip along her legs. The giant wall mirror sent back her image. As an old photograph, for a lingerie brand, she didn't remember which one. Marc, with his camera, who moved above and around her, trying to get from her face the most unexpected expressions. More than ten years ago now. She had not seen him again ever since. He would have been aged. He was some twenty years older than she was. And came that mail, some days ago, she had answered. A phone call afterward. The ex lover he was who was breaking in her empty love life… But his words and his tone of voice were not those of a man trying to revive an old affair. Instead the ones of a man in a hurry who wanted to see her as soon as possible for working purpose indirectly connected, the only information she got from him, to the fields in which they had been linked together. And she even had to urge him to accept that she would come and wait for him at the airport and that he could stay at hers.

She finished getting ready, kept up the Ralph Lauren skirt and top she had decided to wear, but gave up her Pandovans, opted out for lower heels, and dropped the jacket. She made up her mind for a handbag among the tens stuffing her closet, and in it shoved her wallet, her sunglasses, her make up kit and her cell phone that displayed 11.02 a.m. She reckoned that she would need an hour and a half drive to reach Tampa International Airport. His plane was landing at 12.45 a.m. She had some time before her.

Once seated behind the wheel of her 1990 Corvette Stingray, she drove along Lido Key, passed Saint Armand Circle, crossed the bay to the Downtown, went up North, then turned right on De Soto Road and followed the road signs to the I-75. As soon on the Interstate, she revved up and was blown away by the powerful drone of the engine and the steady purr of the tires on the concrete slabs. The swamps and the sparse scrubs that scrolled on both sides of the car made her daydream. She revised some indoor photo shootings with Marc, in New York studios, outdoor shootings too, in Miami and Italian towns. Her face in the magazines, her auburn hair in the floodlights. Sure, she had been very well-known. But to which extent?

As she passed the Manatee River, she realized she had never been recognized in the road. If being recognized in the road was the very determination of a celebrity, then she had never been a celeb, as some of her fellow models had been. Well-known, yes, but not a star. An image in the glossy pages of the magazines that some people had kept in mind, that had determined their way of making up, of hairdressing, of wearing clothes, but not related to real life. How can celebrity be measured? Can we know when no one is there to tell you? Can we be well-known when you do not know it yourself? These were questions she had never addressed, but as time passed by, she now did. Time, and that Florida liquid space that made her feel as if she were floating between a desperately flat land and a desperately clear sky...

Past Bradenton, she had to slow down, leave the I-75 and enter the I-275 interchange. It was a weekday and the traffic was fluid. On the new Interstate, a misnomer since it did not run to the state borders, even not farther on than some ten miles north of Tampa, she could have her motor running fast again. Till she had to stop at the toll of the Sunshine Skyway Bridge.

She loved the bridge, the ballast that threw her up in the air, and, below, these ships that looked like miniature toys. The feeling that everything was meaningless. She opened the roof to be even closer to the sky, and, her hands on the wheel, she looked at the bay. She spotted trails of marine pollution, and remembered that some years ago they could have been a threat to the life of the dolphins. She thought for a while that she had seen one, but the bridge was indeed too high, so that could be. She would have to content herself with their painted effigy on the floor of the airport... In the middle of the bridge, she slowed down as far it was possible. To enjoy the sight and the sun. To prevent the time from running too. She would be ahead actually. After the bridge, she would reach her destination in no more than twenty minutes and she left Sarasota some forty minutes ago. And she did not even think to check if his flight had not been delayed.

When she was again on the ground, she thought she could leave the I-275 and stop by a beach in St. Petersburg. Then, farther on, as she was about to cross the Howard Frankland Bridge between St. Petersburg and Tampa, she more seriously envisaged to go shopping at Westshore Plaza. But she dropped her projects down and reached the airport half an hour ahead. The flight was announced "on time", and she settled down in a bar of the Terminal where she could watch the monorail arrivals and the passengers moving out. Right now, there was a group of tourists from Chicago rushing to board a bus that would take them to visit Busch Gardens and find there that ersatz of Africa that they looked for, and they would find, in Florida.

She ordered a key lime pie and a glass of pineapple juice that she drank with a straw. Then she crossed her legs high on the bar-stool she was seated on.

2.

He was watching the Potomac River that very soon disappeared below the clouds. The plane lightly vibrated, then kept up climbing. He sat up and looked around him. The cabin was half empty. He took a folder out of his briefcase, but had no time to open it up, since a stewardess, arising from the rear of the aircraft, offered him a light meal, which he refused. The girl was pretty, but the United drab uniform, blazer and pants, did not showcase her. He watched her go away, a light from the window inscribed an attractive stripe on her face. She had such a way of walking too...

There were no more clouds in the sky and the coastline was visible, some twenty-four thousand feet down. Was it the Virginia coastline? Or already North Carolina? He knew them both very well, but the altitude flattened everything below and it proved challenging to make one's mind up. He remained for some time watching this coastline that seemed always the same. At last, he did not care anymore and was back to the folder he had taken out of his briefcase. Inside were several newspaper articles, mail paper-copies, and an ensemble of scribbled notes.

He was already entirely in the first article, when an orange flame arose suddenly at the end of the alleyway, close to the pilots cockpit. He shuddered, thought that the flame was going to spread in the aircraft, and blow everything away. No, it only was his imagination. *Just my Imagination*, as in an old Rolling Stones song. The cabin was perfectly calm. Not a sign of fire, even not a sign of smoke. Just to ensure, he looked at one of the rare passengers on his right, half-sleeping in his large armchair.

He resumed his reading. The assassination that had topped the headlines was horrible. In Kentucky, a pretty well-known businessman had been slaughtered in the driveway of one of his residences, as he was about to get in his car. The murderer had escaped, leaving no trace. It seems that he had come out of nowhere before going back to nowhere. No clues. No footprints on the concrete. No motive. The victim had no known enemy. His companies were prosperous and financially transparent. The state police and the FBI had been investigating to no avail. Some points were even more surprising. The residence was equipped with video system. But the cameras had shown no presence. As if they were disconnected for some minutes, even if the analysis of the system could not find evidence.

If it was not in the headlines but in a minor place, the second article was tantamount to the first one as to the horror. It told another assassination, in Europe this time, of the head of a company that was knocked out and killed by several terrible baseball bat strikes on his neck. There too, the facts were disturbing. The act had been performed at the victim's legal domicile, a large apartment in a Parisian wealthy suburb, a little more than a week ago. The murder happened in the evening, as the forensics established it. But no prints were found and how the murderer came on the spot and got out proved impossible to say. Nothing anormal had been observed and only the following day, when the maid came, she discovered the dead body of her employer. His spouse was not there but on their countryside estate. With so few elements, the investigation was doomed to stall and the culprit to remain at large.

The third clipping told about a new assassination, more recent, only some days ago. More classical in a sense, but as disturbing and mysterious. As he was leaving an important meeting, the representative of a big food-processing industry was shot at, from a building in the Brussels European district. Shot in the neck with the arrow of a special riffle, as utilized for the tele-anesthesia of some sort of animals, he did not die instantly. At first he simply seemed asleep, and he was taken to a hospital where he was expected to wake up and to recover from the shock he had suffered. But the next day, his health suddenly worsened. What had seemed an anesthetic turned out to be a potent poison that unexpectedly he died of and that still proved impossible to identify. Some witnesses said they had seen someone rushing into a subway entrance close to the place of the shooting, but as this person could not be caught up and identified, it was impossible to say this was the murderer.

He read his notes again, and he closed the folder. The sky was still apparent. The plane veered very slightly. The Florida peninsula had undoubtedly been reached. An announcement from the cockpit brought confirmation, since the pilot said they were flying over Jacksonville. He looked through the window and saw, indeed, the sprawling suburbs of the first city of the Sunshine State, named after one of the most controversial American presidents. What struck him at first with the three assassinations, was the very absence of any security. The three victims were not, for sure, politicians with personal protection but essential captains of industry who could have been bound, at least, to some precautionary measures. How was it possible that one could get, without being noticed, on the first one's driveway? Or even worse, in the second one's apartment? And how was it possible that the agenda of the third one was so well known that he could be shot when he was leaving one of his meetings? It also was the case for the two other ones. There were, then, other elements, more contingent, but that also disturbed him. The three victims' photographs provided by the newspapers showed some physical similarities. He was for opening the file to ascertain it once again. They represented three Caucasian men, but the unattractive faces with ugly black eyes created, at least for him, a kind of uneasiness. It was possibly the reaction of a photographer used to shoot the most beautiful faces and ocean-colored eyes! Anyhow, this physical similitude was another similitude that perhaps connected the three assassinations. But were they to be connected? There might be no relation whatsoever to establish...

A third point that ensued directly enough from the first one made the three murders closer. Obviously, everything had been very cautiously planned. One had to know when the first one would get into his car, when the second one would be home or when the last one would leave his meeting. It did imply, in every single case, complicity. Terror attacks? Captains of industry and lobbyists had been targeted in the past, already a faraway history. But not Islamic terror attacks. And there was no claim... Some sort of ritual crimes!

Entrenched in these considerations, he didn't notice that the plane had been descending for quite some time, actually after they flew over Jacksonville, let alone that the pilot had announced it, but he surely had not listened. Anyway, they were reaching their destination. In ten minutes, they would have been touching down. On his right, in the windows, beyond the central alleyway, the Gulf of Mexico was shimmering under the sun. On his own side, below the wing, other liquid but land-mixed swathes, all these Central Florida swamps. Before the stewardess came and checked that the few passengers had fastened their seat belts, he fixed his and, well settled in his seat, waited for the plane to touch the ground and the thrust of the retro reactors.

There was still another way of relating the different assassinations. And that was why he came to see Janice.

3.

A dull but violent sound. And the flames that were invading the cabin. Air rushing in. Passengers screaming. And children howling. The plane was going down, then up and down again. He looked at the very entrance of the bay where he should have crashed down, then at Janice thighs, uncovered by the skirt that had flown in the wind when she had opened the sunroof. She turned towards him for a short while, took off her sunglasses, and set them on the top of her forehead to fix her hair. He saw her amused smile and her hazel eyes that, in the blasting sunlight at midday, were clearer than he remembered. When he met her for the first time, she was one of the rare dark-eyed models he photo-shot for cosmetics. An endeavor from the magazines and cosmetics brands to conform to societies in which light-coloured eyes had become, more and more, an exception. Nevertheless, light-colored eyes were still dominant on the beauty pages of the magazines. She used to say that she was proud of the inheritance of this eighth of Indian blood coming undoubtedly from a Mount Shasta Modoc great grandmother…

She was focusing her attention on the concrete when they reached the end of the Skyway. She suggested that, instead of the Interstate 75, they could drive along the coast on Longboat Key. They could even stop on a beach. He had no objection. At the airport, when he showed up in the arrival hall, she did not spot any difference with the man he was some years before. After he got his luggage back from the baggage claim, she did tell him he had aged, but… Even more alluring… He did not reply. And later on, when he sat down in the Corvette, he hardly smiled as he told her he was glad to see her. In the first miles they drove, they did not speak much. She only stressed some changes in Tampa's urban organization while he nodded and watched, impassive, the landscape of the Downtown skyscrappers. But now, she was transported by this male body, just besides her. Something in her had been awakened by this quick look that, at the top of the bridge, he had for her thighs.

They crossed Palmetto, then the first Bradenton suburbs and turned off to the coast. A road fringed with palm trees, and very soon, the Gulf appeared. She slowly drove the Corvette on a scenic drive, at first surrounded by no built lands and then, on the left, along an ensemble of buildings, gated communities, shops, and small malls. Farther on, on the beach side, was a restaurant with several cars on the parking lot. She slowed down even more and parked along them. She asked him if he had a bath-suit, and he told her that, indeed, he had... There were very few people on the beach, and she warned him that she would like to swim naked, but in Florida, as elsewhere in the United States, to the exception of some beaches in California... He added then that there was a time when she and some of her fellow models had posed naked in a New York street.

Finally, they sat down to a table and watched the sea. There was a strange tension between them, a strength that could draw them close or could tear them apart. Two children were playing on the beach, they ran into the waves and came back to snort onto the sand, as dogs could have done. But there was ten years or so that the last beach on that coast that still accepted animals was forbidden to them. "I'd like to see you naked again", he said after a long moment of silence. She thought that he was declaring a desire and she thrush her fingers ahead but, before they touched his, he added: "as on this glorious day". She had often posed naked, but she realized that he referred, now as before, to this advertising campaign she had done for animal rights, flaunting her flesh with three other models, "à poil plutôt qu'avec leurs poils" as rightly said a French slogan. "That's what I am here for". She was not sure she had understood what it meant. But he did not delay explaining it.

He was far more talkative than he had been so far. And under the afternoon heat that made beads of sweat drop along their forehead, she found the far more expansive man she had formerly known. He told her that he needed all the contacts that she and her partners could have had then in the environmentalist movement in general and in the animal rights movement in particular and, he was sure of, she had kept on liaising with. She admitted that it was, indeed, the case and, without asking for his reasons, she agreed on providing the information he required. Then, he talked about the three, genuinely horrible, assassinations, that did worry some of his friends and that he wanted to investigate. She said that the first one, the American one, that was largely covered by the TV networks deeply disturbed her and she turned pale when he described the circumstances of the two other ones she only got aware of, less precisely, through the social networks. He acknowledged that, at first, he didn't really see what the three murders had in common, and, because they had been perpetrated on two different continents, they had a contrasting media coverage according to the countries. Admittedly, there were similarities. A total absence of protection for the three victims, but bodyguards were not necessarily provided to even essential business managers in their professional life, let alone in their private one. A strange likeness in the features of the three men, but it was, he did concede, largely subjective: she might not have the same feeling; he promised to show her the photographs. A minute preparation of the three crimes so that the perpetrators did not leave the slightest trace and were at large. If that last point allowed a better parallel, nevertheless, it was not decisive, chance could be the point.   Another ensemble of elements, on the contrary, was more assertive, and, to him, there was no more doubt that, if the slaughters might not have been carried out by a same person, they were financed by only one organization. The three businessmen were, indeed, the head – or the representative for the third one – of food processing industries while the execution modes were precisely the three main techniques used for the animals which meat would fill in supermarket shelves: throat-slitting, slaughtering, tele-anesthesia. That the first victim, throat-slit, was the head of a company that was killing the animals rather than throat-slitting them and conversely the second one, reinforced the relation between the murders, as if, in reversing two of the execution modes, they became even closer to each other. She listened to him with some form of stupor but with a sort of gratitude. Before he could come to the end of his demonstration, she stammered: "Kind of Eco-terrorism. Animal Liberation Front". He looked at the sea, then looked at her. He said this also was the conclusion he had reached and, accordingly, that was why he wanted to contact animal rights groups. She did not ask who were his friends he talked about, but she was aware that before he became the well-known fashion photographer he still was, he had been firstly, as many others in that job, a reporter-photographer covering, among other things, the Gulf War and some military operations on the African continent.

In the car that, under the sun, had turned a furnace, she switched the air-conditioning on, to the full, and, back on their drive along the Gulf coast, they were silent again. She had straightened her skirt and was focusing again on the road as he, his look lost into the distance, was contemplating the horizon on which, later, the night would fall. They stopped again when they reached Sarasota, on a mall parking lot. She had to buy some pharmacy products. And when they got out, they were dazzled by the sun that, getting down in the West, was sliding on the stucco of the houses, the palm trees, and the car-chromes to create a unique atmosphere. A sly smirk that she noticed was opening his lips.

4.

She could still feel the print of his skin on hers. She considered the bed she had just been leaving. He was still sleeping. She wrapped herself in a dressing gown and felt like getting into the pool to cool down her body, still burning with last night's embraces. But, as she walked through the living-room, she saw the dossier that he had tossed to her in the evening and she had started to leaf through, before... She took it back and went outside and lay down on a chaise-longue. She smiled. She remembered her demands. She had wished that he took her doggy style, and, before he came, she had pleaded that he entered her little hole. His sex was hard, and it was painful, but she was satisfied, after all those months, all those years... Right now, she was almost ashamed of her instincts, of her desires. She thought of Gabriella. She curled up on her seat, tightened the belt of her dressing gown, and opened the dossier.

She went rapidly through the first article she did not learn from anything else she already knew, but dwelt longer on the other ones that were relating events less familiar to her. The weapons which the murders had been carried out with were not that usual and the total disappearance of the perpetrators was as strange as in the American case. She pictured the Parisian suburb where the assassination took place. She knew it well as the Brussels district where the third man had been shot at. Close to the Schumann Roundabout where, as a student, she was on an internship at the European Commission. Yes, Marc was right. It looked like Eco-terrorism, but so far, to her knowledge, animal welfare had never resorted to murder, to physical elimination of leaders of the food processing industry, and so consistently. And no claim had been made to establish it.

Marc was waking up. He turned around in the bed but did not find her by his side. He opened his eyes, and, in the darkness, he did not know anymore where he was. There were flashes of floodlights, naked bodies wrapped around each other, and loud bangs, flames and smoke that rose in the desert. Colored fabrics playing on the bodies, soldiers in military fatigues and weapons that were glimmering in the sunlight, screeching of boots on loose stones. And, by a poolside, a woman with large dark glasses hiding her face. He got up and, lifting the blind louvers up, he saw Janice, who was reading on a chaise longue. She was curled up in a dressing gown and he tried to see the body he had been holding in his arms till the dawn, in vain. Her thighs, long and firm, she had been famous for, were kept inside the blue gown.

He did not move, watching her while she turned the pages of what he knew was his dossier, till he quivered with the air conditioning falling on his shoulders. He noticed the shirt lying on the armchair and put it on. Then he picked up the pants that had been sliding on the ground. Dressed up, he hesitated. Would he join her on the poolside? She seemed too much absorbed in her reading to be possibly disturbed. He decided to go and find the kitchen and treat himself with coffee. He would bring an orange juice to her if he could find a pack in the fridge. But he would find one. Tropicana was born on the Florida West Coast, wasn't it? In a derelict Tampa warehouse before conquering the entire world. One of these success-stories of an Italian immigrant the Sunshine State was crazy for. Ever since, every Floridian had to keep one in the kitchen, even if, lately, unexpected frosts had stricken a harsh blow to the orange trees.

Seated on the poolside with their drink, they seemed, again, like strangers. When he had shown up before her, hardly had she lifted her eyes up, and when he had come nearer and handed her glass, their bodies did not even touch. They had not even talked, as if they wanted to cancel a night intimacy. They retreated in a silence, not even disturbed by the steady whisper of the sprinklers that ended some hours earlier. She stopped her reading at last and looked at him in the eyes. She murmured: "Yes, you're right". He shook his head, and watched a bird, a hummingbird, to land on the deck, at the end of the pool. A slight breeze wrinkled the crystal-cleared water, the only shadow being a leaf that was soon pushed by the stream to the skimmer. They looked at the pool, then the Waterway on which no boat could still be seen. The heat and the humidity were already wrapping everything and keeping them in the silence and the distance of the bodies. Sweat was beginning to drop on their forehead. He felt like taking his now empty glass and throwing it in that stretch of water, breaking its quiet immobility, watching it drowning, shimmering, into the transparent depth. He did not dare. She took a last sip from her own glass, and looked down at him, untying the belt of her gown and revealing her body in the sun. She wished to speak, to tell him not to get close to her, but no sound came out of her lips. She got rid of her gown and left it to her feet. He stayed put, unconcerned, still absorbed in his contemplation of the water.

"I'm gonna call Gabriella", she finally said. He smiled when she pronounced this name. "She will know", she added. He wondered at first what she might know, then he thought that, yes, perhaps, she might know. Gabriella, one of her fellow models, and a very close friend, who had posed with her "à poil plutôt qu'avec leurs poils", and whose involvements for animal welfare were more substantial than hers. It surprised him that there was no animal in her house. He had known her in New York with a cat haunting her apartment. But he was sure that Gabriella was still surrounded by several animals, and perhaps not only cats but more enormous felines. Recently, she had been demonstrating, naked but painted in camouflage gear, in a big European city with a lion cub. Gabriella was at home, in Brazil, she told him, in Porto Alegre, or possibly in Sao Paulo for a week or two. But she regretted as soon that she provided him with information that proved a closer proximity between the two women than he could have imagined. She remembered that, formerly, their antagonism had frustrated some of his projects and that he had had to display great diplomacy to have them work together. Everything, in his view, seemed to oppose them, from their professional rivalry to their sexual orientation, passing through their physical type, Gabriella being the prototype of the Aryan blonde with clear eyes, while she presented some elements of far away miscegenation. Not to mention a birth in the Brazilian and Californian wealth that tended to take them farther away rather than to get them closer. He could not but wonder to learn that they were very close today.

The heat was getting overwhelming. Suddenly, he undressed and dove in the pool. She hesitated for a while but followed him. They swam side by side and ended up brushing against each other, as in an attempt at reconciliation. Then, when they got out of the water, renouncing to dry in the sun, they soon went in. A new brushing of their bodies against one another and the water dripping on the kitchen paving stones, a muesli bowl they swallowed together, then she broke free in the depths of the house in a self-assured and swaying walk that reminded him the model she had been. He was left to gather the clothes and the dossier resting on the poolside and waited for her to get ready.

5.

Annelise de Jager rarely left her hideout on the Cape peninsula. She spent her time watching the ocean and the penguins on the beach of Simon's Town. The travels in her youth that for such a long time had kept her away from South Africa had exhausted her. She only enjoyed some horse riding on the beach, and sometimes a foray in the Karoo she was familiar with in her childhood. Looking at herself in her mirror, she found that she was a perfect summary of the place, with her transparent blue-green eyes, color of the Indian Ocean and her dark hair reflecting the interiors of the dark continent. Yet she was almost totally of Afrikaner blood, the blood of her Dutch and French Huguenot ancestors who, in the 17th century, had settled down the Cape, slightly mixed, more recently, with the one of British colonists who came two centuries later, to whom had to be added a Swedish lineage. Anyhow, she was the white South African woman's perfect incarnation, with a fair skin that turned brown under the warm subtropical sun and her English language, now her everyday language, that still kept the inflexions of her Afrikaans mother tongue.

Standing before the large plate-glass window in ample cream-color crepe pants and navy-blue silk blouse, she was watching the ocean. The living room was still in the shadows, but a sunbeam made its way from the veranda and was shining the handle of a revolver laid on a wooden sculpted table. All that did not bode well, she thought, grasping the weapon and caressing it in her hand. Sure, there were the gated residences, the walls, the alarm, and the cameras but, in South Africa, it still was the best way to stay alive. Indeed, when she had received this phone call, some hours ago, she had been skeptical, and still was. She did not see how the organization could have backed three attacks in Europe and the United States. She considered her naked feet that half disappeared under the hem of her pants. On the grayish stone floor, they looked minor and derisory, signs of her very fragility. But, at home, she never wore shoes and would have wished, outside, never to wear them either, just as in her childhood when she used to run barefooted in the veld. She pointed her gun, at the end of her two jointed hands, to an invisible target in the dark depths of the big room, brushed the trigger, then lifted her arms up and dropped the revolver back on the table she had taken it from.

Her husband would be back soon. She would be waiting for him in her bedroom half naked, or in the Jacuzzi on the terrace that overlooked the bay stark naked. Doubtlessly, as usual, he would like to kiss her and then embrace her, but she, as usual, would reject him. He would stammer some apologies, that he was a cad, and some compliments, that she was the most beautiful woman in the world, and then he would slip away and mind his own businesses. He was short and unattractive, and of British descent, but terribly rich. And, since the time, still recent, of her modeling, she had always made a clear cut between the wealth of her husbands and the beauty of her lovers, not because she was desperate to conciliate the one and the other, but because she did not want to mix them and wanted to respect this distinction made by her francophone African sisters, up in the North West of the continent, between their *grotto* and *genito*. She might kill him one day, even if she had not to kill her two previous husbands, divorcing, twice, after one only year of marriage, and pocketing sums in dollars that, added to the ones, still more important, at the time she was one of the indisputable queens of the catwalk, had left her forever financially set for life. She would kill him, perhaps, a day when he would come back out of the blue and find her with one of her Adonis, sportsmen, models or actors, visiting Cape Town, she invited when he was away, since she could not imagine that he could take hold of the gun on the table and begin firing. Or, even more simply, she would kill him one night when he would come home late, and she would mistake him for a burglar.

That night he came back home late. And he did not find her neither in the Jacuzzi nor in the bedroom, but in black leotard, doing, on a platform of the house, her yoga exercises before going to sleep. Between her stretching and breathing, she hardly noticed his presence. When she was finished, with half-shut eyes she passed him, gave him an open smile and told him that tomorrow she would need the Mercedes four-wheel drive. He asked her if she was going in the Karoo, but she said no, that this time she abandoned him for some days to go to the Amakhala Game Reserve next to Port Elisabeth.

She went to her bedroom where she took her unique outfit off. Gabriella was mad. But she had to check, at least one point. Naked on her bed, she forced herself to think. She relived their years in modeling. They had been very close friends, had been cat-walking for identical houses, photographed on the cover of the same magazines, and had been in the same fights. And more than ten years after, they remained close friends, Gabriella coming, at least twice a year, to visit her in this house on the Cape Peninsula. She would have liked to linger on precise events, linked to their common involvements. But she could not. Instead stood some images of her, images of this woman who, stark naked or scantily clad, had been several times on the cover of different issues of FMH and who had been targeted by all the eyes in South Africa, America, Europe and elsewhere and... by male concupiscence. A photograph of her, on which she was lying down on a leopard skin couch only dressed with a prudish necklace of pearls and she looked at the camera with her transparent eyes, remained for a long time in her mind.

She admired her breast that, hardly hidden with her arms, was bursting under her body and her buttocks that were curving up to compliment a picture that she found so exciting she began to rub her thighs against one another, and to regret that his husband that she heard moving in the bathroom were so short and so ugly. But she chased the image away and, opening her legs and putting her hands on the sheet, palms up, she was able to make her mind go blank. She focused on a point, there in the starlit sky disclosed by the large skylight above her bed.

When she was to fall asleep, she worked out that she would need eight hours or so to reach the Reserve and the Woodbury Lodge. She also thought that she should not forget her revolver. In South Africa, where according to the statistics there was a rape every thirty-eight seconds and a murder every minute, even the Garden Road was not that safe…

6.

Gabriella did not like men. Even Marc for whom she felt a kind of tenderness was no exception to her rule. Him alone... She did prefer women and she remembered that, when she lived in Los Angeles, the media used to depict her, an extraordinary shortcut, as a lesbian activist. But Annelise, the only female she had ever been in love with, had other interests. Accordingly, she transferred her affection on animals, cats, her numerous cats that peopled and furnished her huge empty apartment in Sao Paulo where a big brass bed covered by a purple panne velvet blanket was the only piece of furniture.

She had no car. She had never learned to drive when she was in her teens, even if her parents did insist for her to know. And it was in the helicopter that flew her to shopping at Daslu that she received Janice Dillon's call.

The surname and name of her friend displayed on the screen of her cell phone as she watched below the monstrous conglomeration sprawling as far as the eyes could see, and she was tempted not to pick up the phone. But even if they might have differed in the past on various points, she had no reason not to speak to her since they kept in touch at least twice a week on the social networks and, as the helicopter was descending to the most luxury mall in town, she answered the call. Janice was whispering as if she did not want to be heard. And, indeed, as the aircraft was landing on the mall heliport, she did not listen to her anymore. She would call her back.

  She almost raided two shops. Even if the temperature, in the beginning of the fall, was getting lower, at Lenny Niemeyer she bought the whole collection of last season swimwear. And at Yves Saint Laurent, her favorite brand, she purchased two whipcord pantsuits and several see-through blouses. She complained to a Dasluzette that she could not find that safari jacket the brand had not made for quite a long time and showed on her phone, for educational purposes, that famous photograph of the Sixties that portrayed Veruschka wearing it; she also told her that the photographer, today quite an old man, was living nearby, somewhere in Argentina. She completed her shopping with a few pairs of Havaiainas flip-flops that were definitely far too cheap for Daslu and strolled at Andriana Degreas and Lua Morena. Only when she was seated at Leopolldina for a high tea she thought to call Janice back.

She had to call twice, as the first call failed. Then when she heard Janice's voice, loud and clear this time, she caught herself speaking in Portuguese before breaking off and bellowing an unkind "what's up". Janice did not seem to take offense of her verbal abuse and, level, told her they had to talk serious matters. Marc Fremont was with her, in Florida; he came from Washington the day before and asked for her help. She thought of photographs – the old models were becoming fashionable again – then imagined the pair frolicking by the poolside in the beginning of the afternoon – as on the East Coast of the States it was two hours earlier than in Sao Paulo. But fashion was not a serious matter, as she learned many times at her own expense.

Janice asked her if she could talk and if she was alone. She looked around: there were a lot of people. Nevertheless, she considered that she was anonymous in the crowd and told her that she was alone. Her US phoning person told her then that she knew, of course, about the assassinations in Europe and Kentucky. She did not react, but her silence was as an assent, since at the other end of the line the voice kept on speaking. "Marc has been considering, and I'm considering too, that they might be connected to the AFL". And she added: "What do you think?" She looked at the bags right at her feet that contained her shopping, thought of her cats, alone, in her vast apartment, before she dropped: "Sure, they are".

She expected that Janice would ask why she was so sure and if she knew anything else. But she was contented with reminding her that two leaders of the food processing industry, the American one and the French one, were murdered at home and that a lobbyist had been shot at after attending a Brussels meeting. And she told her that the acts were horrible and a kind of "tit for tat" logic, which were not the methods of the animal rights activists. "I know", she answered, before she whispered: "So far". And she felt like adding that they were as horrible for animals as human beings, but she refrained. Her "so far" left a time of silence, then Janice kept on saying that their actions were so far peaceful and most of the time symbolic, they were both the best examples and privileged witnesses. Very rarely, confrontation occurred. She gave as an only example the recent fights against ships that were slaughtering whales in the Japan Sea. How was it possible they were now going violent? Could she explain it?

    She was tentative. She was about to tell she did not know, but would Janice believe her? She said she did not want to speak now on her cell phone in the middle of a mall. She would get back home, call her back then, or would get back to her very soon another way. She was to interrupt the call when a young bleached haired but white skinned girl came up to her and asked if she were Gabriella Dicker. She answered that yes, she was, and agreed to sign up the tee-shirt that she was putting forward. When she took her phone back to her ear, Janice had already hung up. She watched the young girl walk away, excessively swinging in her white and short pleated skirt, then she garnered her bags and call a bellboy to help her to the elevator and the heliport.

In the helicopter, she watched again the monstrous city below and dreamed the Rio Grande do Sul hills, her ranch where she would get back soon, her animals she would see again. She opened the bags with the two Yves Saint Laurent pantsuits and caressed for a long time the fabrics, until a kind of well-being arose in her. The night was about to fall on the horizon and neon light flashed. She thought she had promised Janice to call her back again when she would be home. Yes, she would explain. She would explain to her why, why the actions that had been carried out so far were not enough. She put the pantsuits back in the bags and waited for the landing on her building roof.

Home, she gave some food to her cats who, as soon as she had been crossing the door, had started meowing, then undressed and lay down naked on the purple blanket of her big brass bed. She watched the ceiling, so white, so glassy, on which she could see the reflection of her body, entirely painted in green, ochre and black motives.

7.

Annelise left early. The garden boy – as she kept on saying, a colonial and Apartheid legacy – had washed the four wheel drive Mercedes, checked the oil and water levels and helped her carry the two Vuitton travel bags to the trunk. She went out of Fish Hoek and drove along the bay. Some surfers, all white boys, were waxing their board on the beach, some others, white too as far as she could judge, were getting ready to ride the waves. She passed on her left the road to Constantia, then crossed Muizenberg and Strandfontein. Soon she was close to the Cape Flats. Although the traffic was sparse, she felt, for ten minutes or so, this anxiety felt by so many South Africans to know they were in the vicinity of the Khayelista and Nyanga townships and that the revolver she had slipped in her belt under her hunting jacket could not chase away. How many times at the end of the segregation era, and to an extent ever since, Cape Town residents had feared that the thousands of poor people and outcasts who were piling up there broke out into the city. But nothing happened and she went north in the interior to join the N2, just before Somerset West.

She drove in the mountains, through passes and began to hum, in Afrikaans, songs that the car radio was playing. Theuns Jordan's *Soos Bloed* and Lize Beekman's *Draadkar Oor Die See* in this case. To her own surprise, for she was not fond of Afrikaner singers and of a language she did not use anymore. The landscape was more and more splendid as she was going on. And she knew it would be again when she would cross the Langeberg. Landscape of mountains, hills, where animals were expected to be seen. But that road was too familiar and, very soon, she did not care anymore…

She reached Mossel Bay, then George at midday. In Knysna, she pulled over to a station to have her gas tank refilled, but she did not even think to ask for something to eat. She had had a full breakfast before leaving and, in any circumstances, she did not eat at noon, an eating schedule she had adopted during her glorious days, and that more recently had turned to total vegetarianism. She only drank some iced tea from the Thermos bottle in the glove box, and she was back on the road. She drove fast on the highway going along the coastline and tried to stop the stream of her thoughts in keeping her attention on a far away point of the concrete. She could not succeed, and had to let images surging, images of her, younger, barefooted, running in the veld or more recent ones that pictured her clad in the most beautiful dresses of her heartbeat designers…

Anyhow, why she was going to Woodbury Lodge did not matter anymore, when her phone, she had dropped beside her on the passenger seat, began to vibrate and then to ring. Surprisingly, for, there in the veld, a connection was not a natural. As she was entering a bend, she groped around for the phone and could not see the caller's name. She groped again, caught it and could press the "Accept" bottom. She heard a familiar "My darling", pronounced with a tone that was not an Anglophone's. She did not need to wait for further words to recognize Gabriella's voice. "How are you doing? Where have you been?"

kept hammering the voice that almost seemed childlike. "I'm driving", she said, while she eased her foot off the throttle and slowed down somehow. "How is it? What do you ring me up for?" She worked out that it was pretty early in Brazil. And Gabriella never woke up before 11.00 a.m.... Suddenly, silence fell upon them and she had to whisper "Hello" to make sure that Gabriella was still on, before, at the other side of the line, her voice said: "I'll be flying to Cape Town next week. Text you when".

She threw her phone back on the seat where she had taken it from and, as during the call the Mercedes had almost been freewheeling, she stepped again on the throttle to go full speed and leave behind a car, she just noticed it in the rear-view mirror, that came dangerously on her tail. Then she realized that next week would come soon as it was already Thursday. Gabriella's morning call took her by surprise, and her next unexpected visit to South Africa did worry her. When, the day before, David had called her up and asked that she come and meet him in the Reserve, that they needed to consult and, perhaps, to take the precautionary measures they had to, she thought, indeed, that his call did not bode well, but she did not take it all seriously. Now, there was Gabriella's call and, if she did not mention what she would come next in Cape Town for, she was more involved in the animal rights organization than she was. She was only militantly against the poaching of rhinos and elephants, the trading of their horns and tusks, or the programmed extermination of the lions, leopards, and buffaloes, South Africa's "Big Five", and if this organization had diverse networks, she doubted that these networks could have any relation whatsoever to the American and European assassinations. On the other hand, if she had embraced, when she was very young, the cause of the animals, she had not posed naked for it as Gabriella and had not even shown at the time, on that issue, a total solidarity with the other models.

She had hit the road to Port Elizabeth for other reasons. David was an ex professional polo player from Argentina who had taken over, for some years, the sales department of the Reserve and the Amakhala Lodge, and she found in him a stable point in the trials of her love and sexual life. Neither *grotto* nor *genito*, but somewhere in-between. Some years older than she was, he protected her emotionally if not financially and satisfied her physically if not sentimentally. And now she wished to see him very soon and to be arriving. She accelerated even more and drove several bends, on the verge of getting out of the road, the car tires screeching. She was driving dangerously and ended up to a more reasonable speed. Two hours later, she was approaching Nelson Mandela Bay, as was called now Port Elizabeth agglomeration. But she would have to pass it, then get away from the coast and follow the N2 eastwards, for an hour or so.

Her thoughts concentrated on the great man, the Robben Island resident who became president, to whom she was introduced when she was a well-known top-model, and her meeting with triggered, strangely enough, her love and practicing of Yoga. Then she thought again of Gabriella. Why did she return to South Africa when her last visit was a little more than three months ago? What role did she play? She knew David, for sure… Gabriella was mad, but… She would have told her.

8.

Marc went back to Washington in the early afternoon and Janice was watching photographs he had just e-mailed her. Corpses of the victims, photographs that seemingly came from forensic institutes. She wondered how he got them. They were really appalling. The first two photo shots especially, the one that showed a throat cut from ear to ear and the second one a neck so much damaged that the head hanged down, inert. The features of the last victim were fixed, but, on the contrary, they displayed a kind of serenity.

She took in the dossier that Marc had left to her the three victims' photographs, published by the newspapers. Surprisingly, they rather seemed like mug shots of criminals. She had not answered when he had asked her if she did not find some similarities to those three faces. But now, yes, the likeness was unmistakable. These same black eyes. But why this likeness? What did it mean? Didn't all the murderers look alike, since the physical appearance is revealing the inner being, according to that old nineteenth century discipline, the physiognomy? And they were targeted, precisely because they did look alike? Yes, it could be. But those black eyes. As if… it was hard for her to express … a minor species was being eliminated. But it might be her personal hang-ups, namely her Indian blood, that she was introducing where they had no reason to be introduced.

She went out in the garden, walked a few steps on the driveway where she had left the Corvette after she drove Marc to the airport, Sarasota-Bradenton this time, in late morning. She felt like sitting inside again, and, in the dusk that was falling, to drive randomly, as if she were in L.A. But the Florida freeways were not the City of the Angels ones and she would not feel, going southwards to Fort Myers or northwards to Tampa, this bliss she had experienced, once, to pass, with no precise destination, from the San Diego to the Santa Monica or to the Santa Ana freeways. She gave up and just sat down on the car hood, this hood she was photographed on, years ago, in an asymmetrical black dress that launched her modeling career. She stayed there for a while, thinking, then came back into the house.

Gabriella, the night before, when she called from a particular device, had recognized that the cause of the animal rights they both had joined had recently been going in new directions that could even develop into spectacular actions. But she did not know what had been decided and if the assassinations were part of them. The organization had very diversified networks, sometimes relatively autonomous and active... She promised to get better informed... Her almost total indifference to the acts and her absence of compassion for the victims were indeed strange. But Gabriella had never been much emotional to external events and had always kept, under a seeming Brazilian relaxation, a deliberate coldness. Even if, in the circumstances, her detachment was nevertheless intriguing. As if, perhaps, she wanted to conceal something...

She switched again her computer on but did not wish to see again the photographs that Marc had sent. She wanted to look at photographs of her, as the one on the Corvette hood. Part only of her fashion photographs were scanned. The other part was in different issues of fashion magazines piled up in her office and other rooms of the big house, with no real chronological or thematic ranking done. But she knew that the Corvette photoshot was part of the scanned photographs. She also knew that it was not Marc's photograph. She had no difficulty to finding it, and remained for some moments contemplating it. Then, she started to slide show advertisements of big brands for clothes, accessories and lingerie, without lingering on one in particular, till she reached the famous one for which, on this glorious day, Marc had made her posed, naked, with Gabriella and two other models, to oppose the use of animal furs in fashion. The shot was indisputably beautiful, but she thought, looking at it, that the French slogan with its "plutôt" was actually shy since, far from encouraging unrestricted nudity, nudity only was a stopgap to the wearing of furs, and it told a preference for a dressed body to a naked one... At the very beginning was clothing... This photograph was but an introduction to other pictures for which she had herself posed as nature intended or, at least, very scantily dressed for fashion magazines or charm magazines, the former with a predominantly female readership and the latter, on the contrary, that addressed almost exclusively male readers. One of them drew her attention, since she was not alone but, between two other girls, Gabriella and a close friend, Annelise, a South African model, that she had been working with on the catwalk without really knowing her. She could not remember when it had been shot and which magazine it was shot for. Marc if he were the photographer, but it was unlikely, could tell! The trio was insistently, almost stubbornly, looking at the objective. However, the two other models' blue eyes challenged this group spirit and she found out that something was frightening in that clearness that put her aside…

The slide show kept on scrolling with much more erotic images, but, this time, they were personal material, photographs that she shot in her own cavorting, without always telling her partner. Some were rather funny, others exciting. But she got rapidly bored as if they were sending her back to the current drama of her love life. After the strange conjunction of the bodies that first night, Marc and she had but avoided each other all day long, putting a distance to a possible and new physical rapprochement with an improbable but true intellectual complicity. And the second night, they sensibly slept in separate rooms, stuck to their computer screens. Yet, he would come back very soon in Florida, no doubt for much longer, and they had decided, on common ground, that he would settle down in her house.

Now the night had fallen, and she remembered what Gabriella had added with a mysterious voice before she hanged up. "A woman is living with animals in the bush, in the heart of Africa. I think I knew her. Met her once". This woman, who lived with animals in the bush somewhere in the heart of Africa and that Gabriella thought she knew was on her mind for already twenty four hours and, she was sure, would remain for a far longer time.

9.

Two points in the dossier were so troubling that Marc had decided to stay in D.C. and not to go on a quick jaunt to New York as he had intended to.

The first one was this absence of prints in the American case as in the Parisian one. He had doubted that it could be total and thought the media had sold it that way, but all the people he knew in charge of the inquiry had assured him that it was definitely the case: no prints. He had been looking for explanation. And it was relatively easy to find some without resorting to outlandish elements. The absence of footprints on the driveway and in the apartment only meant that the terrorists, as he called them now, had taken some precautions, using, for instance, special shoes as the ones used in some factories for self protection, including the slaughterhouses – or even coveralls. Since they had escaped with the weapons they had performed their murder, obviously a butcher knife in the first case and what had been identified by the marks on the victim as a baseball bat in the second one, there was nothing to look for, nothing to find on that side. He confirmed the conclusions he had previously reached, namely that these two assassinations had been expertly prepared.

The other point was even more delicate. He could not explain how, on the one hand, nothing had been recorded on the residence video cameras and, on the other hand, how it had been possible to enter the apartment with such a security system. That the first murderer had waited long hours in the bushes or the second one had come with the victim in his car proved difficult to imagine. As he had been assured that the video cameras had not been switched off, either the tape had to be tampered with utilizing a computer operation he had no idea of but undoubtedly feasible, or was replaced in the minutes following the crime at least before the residence had been cordoned off by the police. In Paris, the murderer had to get the access codes to the building and the keys to the apartment. In short, that implies complicity. But which ones? This question had no answer. Till, as he treated himself with a glass of Bourbon, Four Roses from… Kentucky, an old habit, when he was short of inspiration but already abandoned for some time, an idea came to him… He thought of the two spouses, absent that morning and that night. Strange coincidence. The hypothesis they had … wanted to get rid of their husband was somehow wacky, but was worth being checked… He wanted to know what they looked like. He indeed could find photographs taken in some cocktail party or, at least, those, in the funerals, of two grieving or allegedly grieving widows… He switched his computer on, took a sip of Bourbon, and, when the computer was on, googled the name of the first victim and added "wife" to it. In the "Images" tab, nothing appeared. Only an image of what could be funerals with a woman in dark outfits in the background, so it was impossible to see her features. Only a blonde, almost white hairdo. He did operate the same way for the second victim substituting for the word wife the word "épouse" so he could reach as well the francophone sites. But with even fewer results. No image at all this time. As if the funerals had been done in the strictest intimacy. He gave up the hypothesis he related to his perverted imagination by several decades of photographic creation.

The third murder was less problematic. The *modus operandi* was more classical. But as the other ones it had to be expertly prepared. He did not even consider the conjugal option but rather a well-informed organization as to the doings of the lobbyist. And that mysterious anesthetic that proved to be a formidable poison. He had not, right now, information on, but he would make sure to get some. It could be a way to learn something on the shooter, and even be helpful for the two other assassinations, for he was more and more convinced that the performer was, indeed, one and the same person. It was not only Janice but his friends who enticed him to go in that direction.

For long minutes, he remained bent on his computer, browsing, at random, the most diverse sites. A stream of pictures he could not keep in mind, "Breaking news" that sometimes was interfered, totally insipid. Then he wrote his own name and found the famous photographs of Janice, Gabriella and two other naked models he had shot in the New York streets. But he knew them so well and after scrolling to additional photographs he was the author of, he wrote without purpose this time Gabriella's name. He had no difficulty to find the photograph Janice talked about on the phone the day before and that was not his. Indeed, one of his competitors and nevertheless good friend, for one of those avant-garde British magazines trying, at the time, to question the classical canons of beauty. As long as it was concerned, the shot was no avant-garde at all since the three girls were, on the contrary, partaking in these canons, two of them, Gabriella and the South African model he did not remember to have worked with being even the better example of them. He enlarged it as much as it was possible on the screen. He immediately focused his attention on the latter. Possibly the clothes she wore highlighted her even more, but, to him as to most of his colleagues, the clothes they were supposed to promote had no importance. Only the girl and the context in which she posed were important. And, on that photograph, she was radiant, and so very cute. He was envious of the other photographer that made her so pretty and he did regret not to have known her better.

Today, beauty was becoming suspect and fashion that was to magnify beauty was grim. He thought of the times when he began, some thirty years before. He was aging... Yet, no, he would not have liked to rejuvenate, to make a deal with the devil and to be born later. Inversely, he would have wished to be born a little sooner, so he could have fully lived the Sixties and Seventies when the visual arts and the music had showed, during those two decades, an outstanding creativity that, he was sure, they would never found again. It was indeed difficult to say that a period was better that another, objectivity being challenged then by the subjectivity of the actors. It was perhaps enough to inhabit the present... But, when he came back to his first concerns, which had kept him occupied all evening long, he could but only wonder how it ended up here? How an association fighting for animal rights and, more broadly, for the environment and possibly the future of the entire mankind could kill human beings? And with such odious means? For, while he was now confident that the assassinations were well organized and planned terror acts, he still could not clearly understand the ins and outs.

10.

The next day, it was early when he started working. It was raining and chilly and he craved Florida. But, before going back there to Janice very soon, there were several things he had to be accounting for.

The different investigations stagnated. When the three attacks were not linked to one another and were not regarded as coordinated actions, where, indeed, could they go? And there was nothing he could wait or learn from them. And now, he just wanted to understand the logic of what had transformed a peaceful and spontaneous protest into a violent and coordinated action. Was that transformation inscribed in the history of the environmental or animal rights movements?

Accordingly, he considered, more precisely that he had ever done, the origins and development of the different movements of what he called the Eco-galaxy, through books he bought but never read, or specialized websites. But, most of all, he wished to focus on the first actions carried out by environmental and animal activists that could be regarded as terror attacks.

Eco-terrorism had ancient roots, indeed. It did appear in the United States at the beginning of the Eighties, in the wake of the Californian counterculture of the Sixties and the environmental movements that had been blooming at this time. Some 1000 acts were counted as Eco-terrorist acts carried out on the American soil. The Animal Liberation Front was very active, responsible for half of the acts, so their success had been compared to the failure, three decades earlier, of the German Baader-Meinhof gang and the Italian Red Brigades. Even though it did not refuse weapons and had recourse to hostage-taking, it always took care of not wounding and a fortiori not killing anyone.

Consequently, if one considered that terrorism implied deadly and anonymous actions aiming at civil society, the word might seem excessive for it. The FBI defined, indeed, Eco-terrorism as "the use or threatened use of violence of a criminal nature against innocent victims or property by an environmentally-oriented sub-national group for environmental-political reasons". And even if this legal wording could be interpreted differently, it seemed to him quite difficult it could apply to most of the ALF's actions or it would apply as well to the photographs he took some ten years ago of his models in the New York streets! He thought of Gabriella, her naked body, painted in camouflage mode and her lion cub, or, more recently, of that other naked and ketchup stained girl, lying in another square in Europe, protesting against the use of animal meat.

Obviously, they had reached a higher degree. And if the previous "terror" actions, were fueling, and even calling for, media coverage the last ones were somewhat prone to remain secret. Some environmental activists had spent some time in jail. A famous actress… He remembered, as soon as 1999, a reporter's abduction and detention by armed men who, before setting him free, had branded the three ALF letters on his back. A first warning… The animal cause was not that much a success. The animals to be reared were always poorly treated and in the slaughterhouses the old methods still prevailed. In Africa, the rhinoceros and the elephants were still poached. The big felines were disappearing. Marine mammals too, when they were not used for disputable commercial purposes in the Florida Seaworld and Marineland, and elsewhere. And fur was coming back into the world of fashion. The whole world, as a matter of fact, was going backward. Public opinion was becoming blind. And people had to open their eyes again. But... could such actions be justified?

And who were the performers or the performer? Was a psychological portrayal possible? Were the studies carried on so far applicable? He had read some works on the matter. None was compelling. And they all were outdated. There was Patricia Hearst's case. The Stockholm syndrome as it was termed. He smiled. What an extraordinary story! The grand-daughter of William Randolph Hearst, one of the wealthiest men in the United States, was kidnapped in 1974 in her Berkeley apartment by the Symbionese Liberation Army, a small revolutionary group. She soon took the cause of her kidnappers, fell in love with one of them, and took part in their actions and operations, robbed banks in San Francisco and Sacramento, shot at people in a Los Angeles avenue, planted bombs all around.

Billionaire terrorism. But, after all, that was always the case. No need to call in conspiracy theories… One had to be sufficiently detached from material contingencies to aim at the material world. The animal cause activists, especially, never came from disadvantaged backgrounds. Judging by Gabriella and Janice, their career as a model had made them rich, but they came from very well-off families – which did not help their love life… It was certainly on this side he had to seek, as he had begun to. Nevertheless, he could not picture them with a meat cleaver or a baseball bat, let alone firing a gun with such precision that required professional training. All that was still a man's work.

He could see again this stewardess in the plane that had taken him to Florida, these shadows and lights that striped her face when she went away in the alleyway. Flames and the aircraft that was crashing… A threatening face. The feminine force. But a force that was exercised in other fields that the ones of physical destruction. His investigation made him see the world differently. He did not know precisely how… He did not know who he was. The features of his face in the mirror, when he entered the bathroom, were almost unknown to him. The street, when he opened the blind in the living room, seemed unknown as well. And the strange colored and shaped clouds in the sky as the afternoon ended. Shiva, the Hindu God, destroyer of destruction, or Kali…

11.

When, the following Tuesday, Annelise had been back in Cape Town, she was more serene than when she had left. During the extended weekend she spent in the Reserve, David had reassured her. And her husband was on a business trip in Kenya and he would not be back before a week.

After a very light vegetarian meal that the boy served on the terrace, she luxuriated in the Jacuzzi, watching the ocean, a dark mass on which the lights of some boats were shining. Then she performed her Yoga exercises, meditated for a long time, comfortably set in her favorite fish posture. The vault of heaven up above her and the silence.

Her phone rang, and she made up her mind to go to bed. Her husband wanted to make sure she was back, as scheduled. She told him that, yes, she was back and, as he was worried to think of her all alone, she added she would not be alone long since she was waiting for her friend, coming from Brazil, the next day. Then she hung up. He knew she shared with David the love of horses but ignored, at least pretended to ignore, what their relationship was really like. She could have put him to the test, but Gabriella who would be coming soon had prevented her from doing so. She re-read the message that she texted when she was at the Woodbury Lodge the last night. She was already flying over the Atlantic Ocean and, after stopping in Johannesburg she would land at Cape Town International in the late morning. She thought she might have the time, before she got there, to ride on the beach.

David had reassured her. But at first he fully satisfied her. The first night, in the room overlooking the veld, their embraces were tender and passionate. It only was the day after, when they went on a Jeep getaway in the Reserve looking for animals, that he addressed the other reasons he asked her to come. He feared that the animal rights and welfare organizations could be more and more monitored, and their funding even more controlled. Those attacks in Europe and the United States did worry the government agencies... Some saw in them the mark of the Eco-terrorists. He had no opinion. But if their own organization was not likely to be on the radar, as they focused mainly on the fight against poaching in Eastern and Southern Africa, it had some diverse branches and he did not know all of them, far from it, and it belonged to networks he did not master the complexity of. And her husband and she were essential investors. Then they had to take precautionary measures, and to make some financial arrangements. Primarily, it could be necessary to make more transparent, upstream, the source of the funds and to better check, downstream, their destination. She was puzzled, did not measure well what was at play, then protested against what he had proposed, saying her husband wished to remain an anonymous donor, as well, to a lesser degree as she, and that Gabriella, who was both a significant investor and an active member of their operations, wanted the funds to be easily used, and directed to other actions, if need be. But as David did insist and was persuasive, she ended up accepting his position and promised she would convince her husband.

It would not be an easy job, but it would be even more challenging to convince Gabriella who would arrive the next day in South Africa. She knew she was involved in operations that, as David, she totally ignored the purpose of, in Africa, elsewhere too, and she doubted she could abandon the financial and organizational smoothness the current situation allowed. Moreover, on the road back home, during a good part of it, she had mulled over her friend. She knew her better than anybody else, they had had so many things together, but she had to admit than Gabriella kept a dark side to which she had no access or never tried to have access. She had a phobia of men, but she had never showed love feeling for women, to her own exception, perhaps. She was, in this respect, a kind of blank page… Her anorexia? In compensation, there was this tremendous love she had for animals, especially for the felines. And there was her radicalism which made her support positions that might looked frightening. A youth revolt against a family with extensive landholdings, who had been prospering, among other activities, in animal meat trading. Her sympathies to European and South American terror groups she was too young to have known too...

Could she have been herself an ANC militant if she were born sooner or Eugene Terre'Blanche's AWB sympathizer if she were born later? No. She had often wondered. No, South Africa, or her being away from it for more than a decade, had made her a moderate, at least politically... She did worry for Gabriella, and the idea she would have to face her the next day destabilized her again. She dropped the phone on the table where already her revolver lay and was back on the terrace.

The water was rustling in the Jacuzzi she never switched off and, below, a window in the guard's house was lit up. The sky was clear, and everything was calm. She inhaled for a long time and looked at the bay. A long garland of lights on the land side and the darkness at sea appeased her somehow. She inhaled again and thought of resuming her Yoga postures. She hesitated for a moment. But she finally decided it would not be necessary. She was ready, after all, to face Gabriella. She took the phone and her revolver, checked the security system, and then, slowly but self-assured, she walked to her bedroom.

12.

Gabriella called her from Johannesburg when she was putting her horse boots on. No need to come and wait for her at the airport. She would call a cab. Annelise was not surprised and did not see any matter to ask what her motivations were. She knew her friend was terribly independent. And it was not the first time that she wanted to do it all alone. Once she even arrived unannounced. She only wished that she would not barge in with too conspicuous equipment to attract attention. But she would already have booked her cab and her chauffeur… And she could then ride her horse all morning long.

The sky was clear blue and, in the morning coolness, she galloped more than an hour on the beaches and enjoyed taking her horse in the waves that unfurled on the shore, pressing against its neck, caressing its nostrils. She saw planes going down and turning above the ocean before flying to the airport tracks. Possibly one of those Gabriella was on board. In any case, when she returned home, her plane should have landed, had not it been delayed… It had not, since she only had time to slip out of her riding gear, have a shower and put on black panties, jeans and sweater of the same color when Gabriella called her to say she was arriving.

Some fifteen minutes later, a cab stopped before the property entrance. She allowed the guard to let it in and to open the gate. Gabriella rolled down the rear window and was waving as the car went up the driveway leading to the big house. She went down to welcome her, but hardly had she opened the door that her friend, who did not wait for the car to be in a complete stop, was stepping out and embracing her and kissing her with this South American exuberance that always shook the reserve and distance she had inherited from her Calvinist upbringing. Yet she was sure that something in her had been changing which she soon discovered. When Gabriella's embrace got looser, she noticed she had cut her hair very short. She had never seen her short-haired, and this new hairdressing made her even fairer and highlighted her blue eyes. She had then a martial style even more stressed by the outfits she was wearing, battle-dress pants and a taupe serge woolen shirt, entirely appropriate for a long air travel but that indirectly were a reminder, for they had no more these connotations in fashion, of military fatigues. Anyhow, Annelise did not find this long-haired girl who could have been an ideal type in these beauty pageants South Africa was so fond of and she had herself taken part in a long time ago.

The Xhosa chauffeur, in three-piece suit, unloaded the luggage, two big red Goyard trolleys, but when she asked him to carry them up to the first floor, he showed some reticence to obey. Gabriella noticed it and did not even wait he was gone to express her dissatisfaction for the incompetent and unpleasant airport shuttle services. She reminded her that the taxi war was still raging in Cape Town, opposing the taxi associations and the bakkies. Gabriella did not care and complained about the travel, which had been pitiful in any respect. She had hardly been sleeping in her first-class section with the stewardesses and stewards disturbing her for any purpose and the stop over, in Johannesburg, where she had to take another plane had been even more painful. She suggested that she could rest. But Gabriella declined, saying that, as she should know, she had always been fighting jet lags, at least in the West-East direction, taking on her sleeping time and waiting for the next night.

They settled down on the terrace, facing the bay, but her friend from Brazil did not let them benefit from the soothing virtue of the view. In English with an even deeper Portuguese accent than usual, she told her that she had to get separated from her lion cub who had too quickly grown. David had, definitely had, to get her another one, wherever, in Botswana, if no birth was scheduled in the Reserve, or in South Africa or farther on.

She smiled. She could have invited her to forget this propensity to transform a wild animal into a pet. Still, she assured that David could surely satisfy her wish – she only had to be patient – and took advantage of it, without mentioning the European murders, to talk about the restructuration and transparency measures that the latter wanted to apply in the management of their activities. Strangely enough, she did not object, and even considered they were necessary and engaged to going in the direction he advocated. They just had to discuss the details. Finally, it could prove more difficult to convince her husband...

Gabriella said she already had figured out a name for her new lion cub. She would call him Gabriel, as a double of herself and, mouth opened, she mimed a roaring. As the angel, too... She looked at her. "Great to be here with you... I think you should have one too". Then she leaned over the rail. "Your pool is empty. Why? I want to swim". The gardener had cleaned the basin when she was away, but it would be filled up again before night fall, she said. She suggested instead the jacuzzi on the terrace. "No, I want to swim". The beach was the last option, but at this time of the year, the water could be already cold. Gabriella took no heed of and wanted to go down in town, drive along the coastline and find a place where she could swim naked, swim to the open sea, never come back, get drowned maybe... Gabriella was mad...

Nevertheless, she decided to satisfy her desire, walked in front of her in the hall, and took the keys of her Mercedes from a drawer. When Gabriella saw her take out of the same drawer the revolver she always had with her when she was driving, she shouted: "You have to take me to the shooting range and learn me to shoot. You promised." It was true, she had promised, some years ago, but, never since, Gabriella had reminded it to her…

13.

On Wednesday Marc had returned to Florida. He had been afraid that Janice, as last time, could drag him again in a physical relation he did not want to be dragged into and that she imposed upon him her prisoner mores. But she had not been, neither in the Corvette on their way back from the airport nor since they were in her house, the horny female she had been then.

He was a child of the Sixties and Seventies sexual revolution, and, to him, a good and regular sexual activity was to make sane individuals, and beyond, a rational society. But an aging child, whose sexual desires were beginning to weaken. Fortunately, he thought, for, had he been younger, what the current world was showcasing far from encouraging was somewhat discouraging them. With the Aids epidemic, sexuality had become a dangerous activity in which one had to cautiously engage. At the same time feminism had made the male desire so suspicious that men did hesitate to have it expressed, when they did not totally renounce any expression. The one and the other, with as a background profound social changes, had determined a frightening regression that showed up everywhere and accompanied the return of a morality that one thought was gone. "Epoque calfeutrée par la morale" was the title given by a French fashion magazine to a report of one of his young colleagues. Sure, somewhat erotic images were surging on the Internet, all now labeled pornographic, proof in the language itself that there was no more *eros*. And not only did they consecrate the disappearance of desire they also introduce frustrations between a virtual world filled up with sexuality and a real world where it was no more… Janice was a good example of that… However, it was better they remained in a sage physical distance to one another.

She was huddled on the sofa in the air conditioned living room, dressed in beige silk pants and blouse that highlighted her tanned skin, and he composedly explained where the research he had conducted and his last days pondering had led him. He was convinced, as he had always been, that the attacks were a case for a well organized Eco-terrorism and not, as some naïve press persons had suggested a matter for heinous crime and their quasi simultaneity a case for simple coincidence. But he was also convinced, now, that the three attacks were the works of one and only individual. No objective element could really ground his hypothesis, but he was sure that his very instinct would not mislead him.

Janice called in the physical likeness of the three victims she found surprising, worrying too, and that he had perhaps projected on the murderers. To a same victim, a same murderer or at least a same type of murderer. He smiled, admitted she could be correct, but that such a projection, if real, did not invalidate his thesis, even reinforced it, providing a kind of objective proof that was so far lacking. He confessed that he had been interested in the two first victims' wives but could not find anything, even not photographs. "You're kidding. What for?" she said. But she added as soon that, yes, they could have wanted to have their husbands killed to their own benefit or… because they were militants for animal rights.

That was what he had tried to know… Maybe she could try to get information on her own.

There was complicity, no doubt, he said, in the three cases. And in the two first ones, the spouses could have… Yet the investigations did not exploit this trail. "Far fetched, for sure", but it should be checked. She could take care of it. He also confided in her that the absence of prints could be explained, with special suits for instance. Or the lack of images on the video cameras, in the Kentucky, by a skillful technical handling, but they implied complicity.

He went back to the places of the different murders. Brussels, the European capital where was decided the European Union agricultural policy, where the food processing industry main lobbies met. It was a symbol and the assassination could be regarded then as a political assassination and consequently the two other ones that were linked to it. Paris, the capital of the European state with the most potent agriculture and food processing industry, the most barbarous too. Kentucky was not as strong as a symbol. Chicago with its slaughterhouses could have been a better choice. But the terrorists were simply pragmatists. The man they had been aiming at was a resident of that state, with companies everywhere in the Middle-West. Although... Its horses and the Kentucky Derby Day. And the Bourbon. Indeed not from animal sources... But dope rather that alcohol...

He was going out of his mind... Janice told him. But she could not help finding some logic to his raving. An ensemble of elements holding together. Better fitting together. She was pensive. She felt like she was in a whirlpool. She thought of this woman in the African bush with her animals Gabriella talked her about, as this tale she read when she was a child – Emilio Salgari *The Mystery of the Black Jungle*, she remembered.

He was lying in front of her, dressed in a collarless blue shirt and ample white pants, barefooted, a leg fold under the other that hung in the void. She looked at him, considered for a while his mid long brown hair that had been graying and matched now with his gray eyes, saw the bracelet shining on his wrists, then lingered on his legs and up on his groin. She would have liked to swallow his sex in her mouth, as in the past. But she soon repelled the very idea. She told him:

"Gabriella touched down in Cape Town this morning".

Marc seemed surprised. She said that Gabriella told her about her plan, some days ago, then texted her when she was going out of the plane.

14.

Seated in large wicker armchairs, under the gazebo where they sought refuge in the beginning of the afternoon to find some coolness, Marc talked Janice about the fashion photography newest developments. He was amazed to see more and more animals which he interpreted as a sort of compensation to the turning down by the fashion houses, they both had noticeably contributed to, of furs or other material of animal origin such as leather, or even silk. Since there were no more seals or leopard skin, furs were reintroduced in fashion images through animals promoting clothes devoid of animality. The felines, it seemed to him, were really privileged – he gave as an example the leopard cub in Cartier's advertising – and he was tempted to think that, thus, the images of the predatory big cats at least were revealing the anguish of man before death. He reminded her that the first cave paintings always depicted devouring monsters with sharp fangs… Contrary to many photographers who could be associated with an animal, a dog, to Helmut Newton, he had never photographed animals, even not an innocuous cat. No more than weapons, but it was another story, although…

Janice smiled when he mentioned cats, for she was sure that he referred to her own pet who, in the old days, had watched, placidly, their lovemaking. But she did not interrupt him.

Gabriella did not have those qualms. Even if it was not in shooting of her by other photographers – actually, he did not know very well what it was about – but in her own life. Recently she had been flaunting with her lion cub. And her flaunting, in an animal rights demonstration for sure, could be related, hastily, to other ones… The two prominent examples of similar feline proximity could, indeed, place her in an infamous lineage. The first one was Alice de Janzé, an American woman, married to a French count and in the Thirties a member of the British East Africa's Happy Valley Set, who shot at her lover in a Parisian station before trying to kill herself and marrying him afterwards. And she had been involved, in Kenya, in Lord Erroll's murder. This person already was somehow ominous. The second one was even more since it happened to be Hermann Göring whose photographs with his lion cub in his villa in Berchtesgaden were famous and who had decided to eliminate millions of human beings. They both had ended their life in different circumstances, for sure, the former, after several unsuccessful suicide attempts, shooting herself in the head, the latter swallowing a cyanide capsule after the Nuremberg trial. Murders and suicides, drugs too. Terrible lineage.

"Do you think she ever heard of them?" Janice asked him.

"Possibly".

Marc remained silent and pensive. But after some ten seconds, she interrupted his silence and his musing.

"What are you trying to say?"

He thought over, hesitated for a while, then, almost ranting, declared they were radical personalities, constantly unsatisfied, capable of every excess, nihilists, whose lion cub was a symbolic form for their predatory instincts. He felt she was doubtful. Yet, his diagnosis had no weakness. He could have grounded it even more, put forward that their behavior had been growing on terrible sexual frustrations in the background. Alice de Janzé's case was exemplary, Hermann Göring's one too, even not to a lesser degree. But he dared not propose this analysis because she could also be applied to her and, even more, because he was aware it was the relation, through a lion cub, he was establishing between Gabriella and the two other persons that could disturb her. He was about to tell her that every terrorist, whoever he or she was, had sexual problems, but here, too, he preferred not... In any case, he pursued the Nazis were the first environmentalists.

This time, she approved, nodding. But she objected that did not mean all the environmentalists were Nazis, and he did agree on that point. Simply, they both pointed out when their radicalism tended to totalitarianism. "Or we all should mistrust the ASPCA" she added, bursting out laughing...

She got up, stripped from her tunic, let her bikini slide along her thighs and walked, naked, to the pool. As she was swimming laps in the pool, he came back to the terrorists, or at least the sponsors' profile. It was far more precise now. And even if there were still a lot of persons who could have met the requirements – especially if the sexual dimension he had stressed were considered – the field of investigation was nevertheless somehow reduced... The emails and phone calls were undoubtedly insignificant since they could have been emitted from anywhere. But it was possible to identify where.

When Janice got out of the pool, streaming with water, she walked on the veranda to the wet bar and returned with a carafe of iced tea and two stemmed glasses. She did not take time neither to dry herself nor to get dressed and filled them up with the brown liquid and lay down on two oversized red cushions she had set on the lawn. He took two sips of tea, watched her drinking and adopting an odalisque pose. Some thin droplets still pearled on her pubic hair. He placed the glass in equilibrium on his knee, something she had seen him doing on the sets of the photography studio so many times it had become one of his hallmarks. She admired, one more time, the elegance of that pose and the concentration required and almost did not hear the words he pronounced:

"Have you any idea where Gabriella was at the time of the murders?"

As she did not reply, he reiterated his question.

15.

Janice regularly deleted her emails, but she balked at doing it for her close friends. And it proved easy to find on her computer the messages Gabriella sent her in the last two months. There were a lot of them, two or three every week, but short, and sometimes, in the attachment, a photograph of her or of one of her cats. Some had been sent, if not in the very hour of two of the murders at least less than two days before the first one and less that one day after the second one, so that it was impossible she could have traveled to Europe and the United States in such a short time. Admittedly she might have not sent them from Brazil. It was easy to check. But the content of the messages, even brief, could not make her think they were not.

Moreover, Marc could not really believe that Gabriella could have performed three murders herself. There were too many impossibilities and incompatibilities. On the contrary, he certainly thought she might very well have one way or the other played a part in their organization and their start, as she ended up feeling too.

She was not far from thinking indeed that she had other reasons to be with her lion cub, two months or so before the Parisian operation, on a European square, as she did not spend time anymore on that continent since the end of her modeling, that a simple body painting happening for the animal welfare. Could very well have been planned, while she was there, the European actions, even the American one. Reviewing the emails that she had saved in her box, she could not find any that would have been sent while Gabriella was in Europe, which made it clear that Gabriella, like her, had a rather traditional command of the new technologies and only resorted to them on her PC, in the comfort of her Brazilian residences.

Nevertheless, she felt like forwarding Gabriella's emails to Marc who, in the very beginning of the afternoon, had borrowed her other car, a 2005 Ford Thunderbird, to get to two appointments he had in Tampa, at the McDill base, then in a place on Fletcher Avenue. He would receive them on his iPhone and could have the place they were sent from checked. But she renounced, considering that it was no urgent matter and they could be checked when he was back in the evening.

She wanted to move to something different and to try to get information on the American victim's wife, as she had promised Marc, but, as she got back to the dossier he had left her, another element she had not care of diverted her attention from that. On one of the crime scene's photographs, did appear the car in which was to climb the businessman when he was slaughtered. A Lincoln Continental, a recent model, but she could not but relate it to the one John Fitzgerald Kennedy was assassinated in on November 22, 1963, in Dallas. It might not be a mere coincidence…

She stayed motionless before the photograph, lingering on the Lincoln's radiator grill and the chromes and letting her thoughts invade her. The most mysterious twentieth century political assassination, not yet resolved. Among the most different trails, the Mafia, the CIA and Florida's Cubans, she favored the last one, at least since she had been living in Florida, and she had been a witness of the radicalism of South Florida's Cuban community that still called itself "El Exilio", some fifty years later. The Bay of Pigs. The betrayal of Kennedy they had never forgiven... She remembered, as she was a child, her first visit to Miami in 1980. The Marielitos. Tents on the Orange Bowl's parking lots and under the I-95 in Downtown Miami to take them in... Going back in the past to know or know not... She envied Marc who remained in an enduring present. The girls he photographed were always twenty or so. They adapted to his imaginary or he adapted to their, it did not matter...

The motor grill and the chromes... The blood stains on Jackie's pink skirt suit. She thought of John John on the day of the funeral. John John who died in this plane crash. John John and his girlfriend, Daryl Hannah, one of today most fierce environmentalist militants in the United States, who had spent some time in jail, still punishable by imprisonment... No, there was no link... Then she came back to the murdered man's wife. She found on the Internet the funerals photograph, this blonde woman in the background Marc told her about. She ended up, typing her married woman name, on a new website, only two days old, he could not have had access to. The information was short, only a few lines identifying her, but she only kept one thing in mind: her Brazilian origins... they could have facilitated contacts and affinities.

She was far too excited to develop a narrative, but she wanted now to consider the Parisian attack, find some confirmation... Firstly she did not find anything, neither on the Anglophone sites, nor on the Francophone ones that she inspected without understanding what she was reading, her French having terribly downgraded since her cat walking in Paris. She was ready to give up when she fell on a Dutch site. Better understanding a language she had studied at the university for the sake of finding old family roots and kept up her skills of it on her Brussels internship, she learned that the victim's wife, away the night he was killed, was a Dutch citizen. Then on another site, she discovered her surname and name. And when she googled them, another character, Latin sounding, replaced them with multiple images as the page displayed. She thought she had been mistaking. She closed the application, rewrote the surname and name, to see again the phrase Malvina replaced them. It might be a homonymy, the Malvina's real surname being frequent in the Netherlands and Belgium, but… there was the name. No, there was no doubt. It was Malvina, a model, born from a Dutch father and a Surinamese mother who, in the Eighties, had a career in Italy, embodying in the photographic objective of a Marc's friend… the Sicilian woman. A half-blood woman, she was somehow the heiress of the colored models, who appeared on the catwalks at the end of Seventies. She was some ten years older than Gabriella and she were. An older sister to an extent, she had never met, but she knew and liked what she had been achieving. She did not think she was married to… Recently, surely. She was said to be…

Gabriella would have known her, one way or the other, as she knew the Kentucky man's wife.

16.

She would have many things to entertain Marc with when he was back… The clock on her computer said: 6.32 p.m. The dusk was beginning to fall. He would be back late, in the lukewarmness of the night. She decided to go swimming.

Around the pool, on the Kikuyu lawn, several frogs started to jump. And she thought of those frequent invasions by frogs Florida was the victim of, even more of that one, some ten years ago, in a Fort Walton Beach house. Almost a nationwide event. And the Everglades' alligator that came to deliver in private pools. But the frogs were soon to disappear, and no alligator was in sight. In that region, storms were more deadly than the alligators and the sharks… She took off her shorts and tee-shirt and dived.

She believed that Gabriella had met Malvina in Switzerland, on the banks of Geneva's lake, or Zürich's, unless it was a German or Italian lake, she was not sure. For she remembered, as she was swimming that Gabriella had written to her, a long time ago, in their last years of cat walking, she had met one of their model-icon. But she might be mistaking. They might have met more recently.

However, if they knew each other, they were a strange pair, kind of a chiasmus or oxymoron as the linguists would say, a Dutch woman of South-American descent with dark skin and eyes and a Brazilian one of Germanic descent with white skin and clear blue eyes! Clear blue eyes that she, for sure far less mixed-race than Malvina and of more respectable miscegenation, had envied to that girl from Brazil… As these boys in a book and famous movie, the last one, to her knowledge, starring Gregory Peck, one of her male icon when she was a teen.

The Boys from Brazil… When she got out of the water and dried her long auburn hair, she kept the title of that movie in mind. And, very soon, as she was getting dressed, surged images. She did not think immediately of the ugly-eyed faces of the victims but let her imagination wander to and fro on lost horizons and improbable constructions. Planes that disappeared and men transformed into women, drag queens and transgenders. But when she thought of the three victims' faces, she suddenly understood. It was usual, today, to compare the animal slaughters to the Shoah. Even some great writers had done it, as the recent South African literature Nobel Prize, John Maxwell Coetzee who, in a moving text, insisted on their real identity. Moreover, some Jewish organizations considered it offensive. And she remembered the controversy fostered by a chicken-filled truck going to a slaughterhouse on which was written: *Auschwitz, Buchenwald...* But those three faces that looked alike! As if they were clones of the torturer, no more issued from a superior white race which blue eyes were the hallmark but from an inferior branch of the white race. As if... As if the animals' executioners were all supposed to belong to a determined physical type. Or at least, among them, were chosen to be suppressed those who belonged to that physical type. She would verify the physical characteristics of the most significant number possible of the biggest, and most minor as well, food processing industry leaders. With the Internet, it could be an easy task. She was surprised too by the solidarity expressed through the eyes. Gabriella and her cats, some having beautiful clear eyes as she knew, and those company leaders their eyes identified to the farm animals their work was to kill, before they were themselves killed… by…

She stretched out and sat on an armchair, looked at the water, quiet again, after the whirlpool her own body had cast. No, she was going too far; her last points were crazy! Yet, they had some evidence of those one never wanted to see. Would she tell Marc? What would he say? Under the lights of the garden lamps that had automatically switched on, frogs were jumping again before disappearing into a cluster of tropical plants. She did not care and wondered who had committed the murders that Gabriella sponsored and prepared. A militant may be, or a mercenary paid for the work? Nothing could guide her. She stopped thinking and, stuck in her armchair, she waited for Marc to be back.

He came back late. She did not move from her chair and, almost asleep, did not hear the car's engine, but stood up when the headlights illuminated the driveway and the electronic gate of the garage slid with a soft hiss.

He blamed her for having waited for him and suggested they took stock of the situation the next day. But suddenly excited, she wished they could talk on the spot. In her shorts and tee-shirt under which her breasts were sticking out, hair tousled in the humidity of the night, she looked her best. As an old fashion figure. The one that had arisen his desire. He tried to remember when and how he had desired her, but he could not really remember. Had he really loved her?

She told him about the research she had been conducting on the Internet. She said to him it was unlikely, even impossible, that Gabriella had been on the spots where the attacks had been carried on. But she explained that she was almost sure their friend had been in touch with two of the victims' wives. She elaborated in listing all the elements she had garnered. She focused for a long time on Malvina, that ex top-model whom Gabriella had indeed met and who had become, quite recently, the French businessman's wife. But she omitted to tell him about her subsequent divagations relative to the faces and eyes, for she knew he would rebut and attribute them to her own phantasms.

Marc had listened without interrupting her and had remained silent all the time she had been ranting – he had simply pouted when she had come to Malvina.

"Good job, he said, when it was over. Everything fits with what I learned this afternoon".

Then, on the lighted poolside, he helped her out of her armchair she had stayed on and, walked her slowly inside, in the living rooms, then on the big stair, to her bedroom.

17.

His French was too basic; he could only say some words as bonjour or au revoir, and it was in English he was speaking to the staff of the Golf Hotel where, a little more than one year ago, Alassane Ouattara, his supporters and inner circle were still residing before he became the president of the Republic of Ivory Coast. The hotel had been refurbished since, but as the Hotel Ivoire, the other Abidjan's upscale hotel, it had lost the splendor of the time this West African country was regarded as Africa's Switzerland. In his room, the air conditioning was on, drying the more and more humid heat at the very beginning of the rainy season. Nonetheless, he aspired to go back to the dryness and coolness of the East Africa's highlands, before he could reach his final destination.

Fortunately, he was going away the next day. He looked at his plane ticket. The departure to Nairobi was scheduled at the afternoon's end with a, strange, stopover in Kigali. A new red-eye flight, longer, even more grueling than the one from Frankfurt to Abidjan... He had, now to book a cab. Still judging by the time it took in the morning to get from the Port Bouet airport to reach the Golf Hotel, at the other end of town, with gigantic traffic jams on the bridges and the boulevard along the lagoon, he would have to leave the hotel in the beginning of the afternoon. He did not have any luggage, only a tiny bag with a change of clothes, so tiny that, on his first flight, he was even allowed to keep it in the cabin. It was far more logical and shorter to fly directly from Europe to the East Coast of Africa, but he had to take precautions, to cover his tracks as much as it was possible. When he had left the United States, he had already reached Europe, flying through Mexico, staying then in five European countries...

A Rhodie's life, he told himself, doomed to run away from the country he was born in, to deny the one he had been welcomed in, and run away again from the one he was a resident and a citizen of. He decided to go down to the reception desk and book a taxi, then to have dinner, even if it was early.

He only had to book his taxi the following day, and in any case, the receptionist said, there always were taxi men waiting before the hotel. It reminded him that African nonchalance he had forgotten and he did not insist. He wished he could have dined outside, but the humidity held him back and he sat in the dining room close to the plate-glass window. From where he was seated, he could see the swimming pool surrounded by sculpted elephant-like rocks, one of the interests of the place and the country's symbol. Where he was born, at the beginning of the Seventies, the elephants were rarer, and today at risk of extinction, because of the poaching of their tusks. There still were the leopards, in a marked decrease, too, for other reasons. He relived his childhood landscapes around Salisbury, the bush and its colors, the marvelous clouds, and the blooming jacarandas. He remembered the Meikles Hotel his parents took him to for dinner every Saturday night. As the Golf Hotel, it still stood but had lost the aura it had had then, before and after his birth, at the time of the UDI. The only time he returned to Rhodesia, at the beginning of the 2000, it found it dirty and sordid.

A whole lot of white people were gone, when the "terrs" as they were called during the war, had come into power, when the United Kingdom had them betrayed... Some had stayed, strengthening, sometimes, substantial fortunes and offering safaris to billionaires... A childhood girlfriend, close to the royal family... But, contrary to many other Rhodies who had settled down South Africa or Australia, they went to England, then, soon, to the United States, the East Coast and the West Coast where his father had been thriving and was still thriving... Selling weapons to other African countries...

He dined alone, sending back the white livery and golden buttons waiter possibly from Ghana who invited him in English to have more that the thin plate of vegetables and the tea he had ordered. In his khaki chinos and his linen shirt of the same color, he almost felt out of place, as if the masters were now the slaves... A fair return of history... He thought of the "Abacost" movement, in the decade he was born, by several African leaders in Francophone Africa. They refused with this term the suit and tie of the European and American politicians they regarded as a symbol of Western imperialism. There had been some quite quaint outfits such as the open-collar jacket and the leopard cap of Mobutu, the president of Zaire. Yet, the great majority of African men of power were not only fond of the Western suit but were parading under the tropical heat in three-piece suit, when very few Europeans or Americans were wearing it. Three African hotel executives who rapidly showed up on the reception side before disappearing in the corridors gave him a perfect illustration of it… It was not a paradox as it could have been regarded as but it only witnessed that Africa had gone from colonialism to Neo-colonialism. He thought again of Rhodesia, that black country governed by white people, the "bread-basket of Africa", as it was called at the time, today one of the planet's poorest countries. "No doubt that Cecil Rhodes is turning in his grave". This grave, The World View, he had visited in the Matabeleland once.

That black country, governed by white people… As the Amahaggers' one by a white queen, in that Rider Haggard's novel that, the first time he read it, had kept him awake a whole part of the night, in the boarding school he was studying in. Ever since he had always related to, as a form of fiction in reality… He watched the rock-sculpted elephants in the park again. The wind was rising and a storm would soon burst into the sky.

He insisted to pay in cash, as he would pay for his lodging, the next day, and was back up in his room. A South African businessman had already paid for his hotel in Nairobi, for as long as he wished to be there. He would have nothing to care about. Only sleeping, then going to the airport, under heavy rains, maybe, that were beginning to fall. When he took his toiletries out of his bag, slid on the room desk a black and white photograph of a gorgeous woman, in battle dress pants, on a savanna background. He put it back in the bag, with his travel papers.

18.

The plane was on time, almost an exception in Africa, and after a somehow tumultuous boarding, when a horde of women dressed in colorful boubous rushed out in the plane alleyway, he sat in his first-class seat. As far as he could judge, he was the only white person on board. He waited for the take-off and watched the lagoons disappear under the wings when the plane climbed into the clouds. Abidjan looked like an American town, maybe not those he had crossed running away westwards, but surely Miami or Jacksonville he hardly knew.

    He remembered the cars he had rented, two sedans; he had not cared which brands, the first one in Louisville, the second one, some hours later, in Saint Louis. The road had been extended, and monotonous, to Cheyenne, in Wyoming. He only stopped for gas, in somewhat deserted freeways rest areas, and slept on the backseat in the same places. A local farmer's daughter at the station's cashier, somewhere in Nebraska, whom he held his dollars to tried to strike up a conversation, but he declined politely without his precipitation looking suspicious. Then things got better. He halted in a Dubois hotel, slept longer and then reached California crossing the Idaho and Nevada majestic landscapes he had learned to love in his youth. On the endless highways of the West, he felt safe, the immensity of the place becoming a protective cocoon. When he stopped in town, he was looked at, especially by women, but there was nothing to be afraid of – he had been used for a long time to attract female eyes. In Los Angeles, everything had been rapidly done. As planned, he saw nobody, rested for some days in his Laurel Canyon's house, where, a decade or so ago, he had stayed with Gabriella, then at LAX had boarded the first plane of the day to Mexico where he had flown from in the evening to Europe.

The night was already falling, and the plane flew, slightly bouncing, to the center of Africa. A trip to the center of everything, he thought. That did not mean Africa's anteriority as the first place where human being was born, somewhere between the Kenya and Tanzania highlands, a golden age where one was living in harmony with nature and animals, he simply thought of Rwanda where they would only touch down in eight hours. The origins of the Egyptian Pharaonic civilization for some, as the Senegalese historian Cheik Anta Diop the university of Dakar was named after, his Rhodesian countryman, Wilbur Smith too. Those Hamitic populations, as they had been called in the nineteenth century or Nilotic as they were called today, could have sailed the Nile down to its delta. He thought of those Afrikaner families too, who, as he read in a recent book, after the Boers wars, would have run away from the British-dominated South Africa and with their oxcarts would have gone North to finally settle on a farm close to the Mount Meru, as many proud and irreducible white Masais, with a slew of remaining descendants.

From time to time he dozed off. But when he was awake, he resurfaced most recent parts of the black continent's history. There were those Belgian refugees who had left the Congo, after independence, and had increased the Rhodesia's white population. He had not known any of them, since they soon left, but, during his childhood, in Salisbury, narratives of their exodus were still circulating and, in Brussels, he had stayed at the Plaza Hotel where had been signed at that time the Congo Declaration of Independence, while Grand Kallé sang *Independence Cha Cha Cha*. The African Jazz, the Congolese Rumba... He remembered that rock group, white Rhodesians, The Otis Waygood Blues Band, who had introduced him into the music world... And there was the Rwandan genocide, a tragedy born in an ancestral rivalry between the Tutsis and the Hutus, that was indeed reinforced by the Belgian colonization, that had privileged the former, long-legged and thin-nosed nomadic shepherds whom the nineteenth-century racialist theories had even given white origins, to the detriment of the latter, negroid and flat-nosed sedentary agriculturalists. A sequel of massacres that had no end, as... He would not go out of the plane in Kigali, and could not have a look for himself, but he wondered how these two groups could still be living together. When they would take off to Nairobi, they would fly over Uganda where, after the independence and the Hutus' taking power in Rwanda, many Tutsis had found refuge and where from they might have planned the attack against president Juvénal Habyarimana that had launched the 1994 genocide. Uganda where Idi Amin Dada threw his opponents to the crocodiles and who was said to be a cannibal. His parents and their friends, he remembered, used that story to justify the white supremacy of the Rhodesian Front's prime minister, Ian Smith. And to think that some wanted to settle down the British East Africa Mau highlands, in the beginning of the twentieth century at the time of Thomas Herzl and Zionism, with a Jewish community that could have turned into the State of Israel! The Uganda Proposal as it was called, in fact instead on the current Kenya territory than in Uganda… He also thought of the Tel Aviv bound flight hijacking by Palestinians joined by members of the Red Army Faction and the Israeli army intervention that had precipitated the dictator's fall. Actually, he only was keen of it, years later, through the movies made about it. With a genuine fascination… The State of Israel was the only State to have recognized Rhodesia's independence…

In the aircraft lavatories where, later, he sought refuge, splashed some water on his face, and got fully awake, a passenger had left a contraceptive pill box. Forgetting those pills did seem very meaningful to him. Meaningful of Africa and its demography, seven or eight children to a woman, which compromised all the development opportunities. Africa where Aids decimated entire groups of people but where, nevertheless, the population kept on growing exponentially. The white people's civilization, he was on this plane, the only specimen of. As these lavatories... But according to a proverb he ignored who had authored, a white man in Africa would always be as a Jew elsewhere. Except...

He returned to his seat, tried to see the land through the window on his left. But the night was black, desperately black. But terribly calm too. They might have been already flowing above the immense Congo. He would have to wait for two or three hours, before they reached the thousand hills country, at dawn.

19.

The South Africa businessman who was waiting for him at Nairobi airport, on this late Saturday morning, was short and ugly enough, but his ugliness was tempered by his blond hair. Unlike these three men... he killed. Nevertheless, he was surprised that Annelise had married him. A marriage of convenience and patrimony, Gabriella had told him.

Annelise's husband gave him the keys to a car parked in the airport parking lot, a gray last model Range Rover, a cover name voucher to an upper-class hotel, road maps, and a briefcase filled up with banknotes of local currencies; in the middle of which an automatic Glock pistol with several ammunition boxes had been slipped in. He told him he did not know who he was, where he would go, and what he would do, and he did not want to know. So that he renounced, when they parted, to ask him, as he was firstly intent on asking, to greet his wife for him when he would return to South Africa…

He checked that there was in the car trunk the radio equipment he had required and on the backseat, a second spare wheel; then, after he had fixed up the vehicle seat, and got used to the controls, the wheel on the right side, the clutch on his left hand, the accelerator and brake pedals, he headed for the Kenya capital town center – one of the world most dangerous cities according to some statistics. He weaved in and out streets and finally found his hotel, the Stanley, more rapidly that he had imagined he could. He checked in, followed the bellhop in the corridors, thanked him when his bedroom door opened, put his bag down on the bed, and introduced the briefcase in the wall safe he struggled to close. Then he took two towels in the bathroom and went to the pools.

A life by the pools, he might have been destined to since his first steps in this world. As far as he could go back in his life, there were those turquoise-blue surfaces that had determined who he was and who he would be. On a poolside his father had told him they were leaving Rhodesia, then renamed Zimbabwe. It was on Long Island's poolside he had his first contact with the United States. It was on a poolside when he was a UCLA student an agent had spotted him and asked him for modeling, it was on a poolside he had met Annelise and Gabriella, it was on a poolside the first ALF's feat of arms had been imagined, it was on a poolside that... And he had indeed forgotten... Less important or, on the contrary, even more important ones...

Yet, his life could have been different. He could have become a social scientist, but his physical appearance did not fit. When he was writing his Ph.D. in political science he never finished, he had soon felt that he was atypical, and he had understood that intelligence did not go well with beauty. He could have become a wealthy businessman, but his father had been before him. And he was, in any case, his only heir. He finally preferred to live with a beauty and a wealth that were innate, and he had not to fight for. Sure, he had not been a top model – could a man ever be one? But he made some money in the only job women made more money than men. Nor had he been a great entrepreneur but had helped his father to grow his wealth even more.

And he had very soon this commitment to the environment cause and later to the animal rights. As to the former, he was simply participating in a California tradition that originated and developed in the Sixties counterculture, in the wake of those who had established the first Earth Day, Gary Snyder and their ilk. As to the later personal reasons played an important part. His African background, firstly, for indeed being born on the African continent, identified as animal continent, made him more caring for the animal welfare; secondly, and some could regard it as a paradox, his own involvement in arms trading and dealing, for, in an American, rather than African traditional way, he had spent time since he was a young man in shooting ranges and with hunters.

He had never shot at animals, but he had seen, in Africa as in America, the respect that their executioners paid to them. He remembered that, somewhere in Louisiana's bayous, the deference, a young Cajun who had taught him to shoot with a long and heavy rifle used for crocodiles, even showed for the reptiles. More sophisticated sociological inquiries had confirmed his own observation, making clear that most of the time the hunter's imaginary was far more an imaginary of fusion with nature than a bloodthirsty warrior's one. But if he had felt a kind of sympathy for the hunters, he had soon come to detest animal abuse in the extensive processing food industries. And, as he was shooting one of his last advertising's campaign for a well-known jeans brand, he had approved the ALF actions, as the hostages-taking, then one of the hostages' branding with the group initials. His activism had even gone tougher since and along some other activities that got less media attention, he had encouraged his father's company to get tele-anesthesia guns to alleviate the suffering of the animals in the slaughterhouses.

He ordered an ugali dish and his usual cup of tea from a waiter who looked like coming out of the colonial Kenya. The Kenya's big hunting parties. Hemingway's and Karen Blixen's Kenya and some others. The Masais' Kenya too. He could see old photographs of that time, pictures of rifles and hunting trophies, and he thought of the big butcher knife he had taken care of cleaning and throwing in the Mississippi River, of the baseball bat he had cut into parts and had gotten rid of into a dumpster then spreading the sawdust into the wind, of the rifle he had taken to pieces, put them back together in another way and integrated in his company's orders... No trace. The purity of the origins... The victims. They had no right to live. No more than he had, perhaps...

The waiter brought on too large a tray his maize and tea. Only then did he notice the sky was crowded with clouds, and he was alone... by a poolside.

20.

He had only known one woman. Unless he had known so many he did not remember. As if they had never existed. The next day, when he woke up, it was what he thought.

He had been and still was, one of the most beautiful men of the world, as it was said sometimes of him. In any case, he was a very handsome man, and women had desired him so much he could not say no or, on the contrary, he had them all repelled. Men too. He did not know anymore.

His beauty had been his own burden. It could not be combined with other things. He remembered that one night, it was already a long time ago, a female friend who did not know how exactly wealthy he was, had told him: "You're a very handsome man, and you're aware of it, and you're very smart and brilliant, don't you want to be very rich as well? That would be far too much. Please no more very". Beauty was at odds with intelligence and maybe with wealth too. He had understood it at the university when he had given up his doctoral studies to get into the, feminine, universe of beauty. He had understood that beauty was the prerogative of women, only their prerogative. It was inscribed in the language, in every language: the fair sex, le beau sexe, das schöne Geschlecht, il bel sesso... And if woman were the fair sex, it follows that man was not and that he could not find his place in the beauty territories. He was something else, warrior power, financial power, intelligence, and knowledge, according to the time and societies. From this fundamental dissymmetry so many representations were induced and developed in as many social constructions! And those representations were holding on... No need to call in the famous saying that a woman had to be beautiful and keep quiet or to focus on what a poet wanted to say, claiming you have to be a fag to love an intelligent woman; it was the facts that, the more a woman is pretty the more she is feminine until she is rejected into stupidity, as were today those the blonde color of their hair is another major aesthetic and feminine characteristic…

The male model he had been was no more than an institutionalized gigolo of the catwalk. Moving about in the feminine territories of beauty, he could not be but feminine, as far as the face was concerned, if not the body. But, because he moved about in those very territories, he could no more have the financial power, traditionally hold by man. He only could be opposed in any respect to the man intellect and rejected, as her blonde sisters, into stupidity.

Yes, his beauty had been his burden… As Africa had been the white man's burden once. He had been trapped into the feminine and his rebellion, all his rebellion, came from that… From those long-lasting representations. From the sex and gender prison. He might not have known only one woman, but he had only loved one. And yet this one was born a man. And he was heading to her… He could have turned himself into a woman, too! Since he was woman through his beauty, better totally be that woman! Yet, he had never considered these sex changes that in the Greek mythology almost conferred on Tiresias, the soothsayer, an immortality, and that, in some ancient rites, got closer to the Gods in annihilating time and space. He had even refused when he was suggested to replace in a show Gabriella and, made up, to promote women's clothes. His masculinity resisted… He had only reinforced it…

He only had one photograph of her, he always kept with him, but he kept in mind those Eighties photographs, almost forgotten, in which she was posing in the Sudanese savanna for up to date brands a tiger by her side, or sporting local ethnic war paintings in the middle of bush fires. No more did he forget these other photographs, not as old, for which an American photographer had juxtaposed, with a shrewd montage, one of her poses as a Hellenic antiquity goddess with a today South Sudanese model's ones. Almost a synthesis of Leni Riefenstahl's work who, while she had been the eulogist of the Aryan beauty, turned into pictures the beauty of the Nuba, Shilluk and Nuer, the region's ethnic groups. He remembered that her album had been released, after years, and years of work, when he was just arriving in England. All Hamitic or Nilotic ethnic groups by the way. As if, when one tried to escape the white beauty's codes the Western world had imposed on the whole planet, they were to be found among the black people closer to them. The fashion world was the best possible illustration of it. The black models, when they appeared on the catwalk at the end of the Seventies, came from the East Africa Hamitic population, as the most famous of them, the Somali Iman, and kept on coming from there ever since.

That is where, or beyond, she was living today, and he would go and find her among the animals she loved. He had no watch, had never worn any and got rid of his cell phone months ago. He could have switched on the TV set he guessed the dark shadow on a chest of drawers. But he preferred to call the reception desk. 1.00 p.m., they said. He had slept for more than twelve hours... He opened the curtains up. The sky was still cloudy, and the temperature would be cool. He did not know if he would go out of his room or ask for his meals. He would stay in Nairobi for some days, then he would hit the road.

21.

Janice was now convinced that the man who had executed the three captains of industries, in Kentucky, Brussels and Paris was close to Gabriella or that he was a member of a group close to those that Gabriella attended or had been attended. Her point was simple. If at least two of the victims' wives had provided her Brazilian accomplice with all the information on their husband's habits and the means to access their residence, it seemed obvious she had them transmitted to someone she worked with. A hitman could have been hired for the occasion, but she did not buy it. To such an action, one had to be deeply involved in the cause, to be an activist, a tough guy…

Marc agreed with her diagnostic and encouraged her to investigate in that direction. During the weekend, they did not move, and while in the garden under the palm trees' shade, he had phone calls and talked to interlocutors who, she was sure of, were unlikely to be related to the case; she tried to list all those who had resolved around Gabriella and her, when they first had committed to animal rights.

There were plenty of them. There was Marc, of course, the "a poil plutôt qu'avec leur poils" photographer, other photographers, producers, advertisers, make-up artists, hairdressers, designers, and journalists too. Still, she did not know all of them and had even forgotten most of the names if she had ever happened to know them. There were ordinary people too, autograph hunters… And some girls, like Annelise, who were close to Gabriella… She had kept the videos of their shows and felt like seeing them again. They all might be available now on the Internet but she fetched an old VHS VCR, she had fortunately kept in a cupboard, and with the pleasure of the old time regained she watched them one after the other.

Finally, fashion had not changed that much. No fur, no leather, but synthetic, for sure. But already in these times, overlapping or interlocking outfits, colors that poorly matched or did not match, different declination of long, short, masculine-feminine, frills, close to the skin, draped, black, white, golden, and green that the magazines could not synthesize for every season and they simply listed in a supplement, an admission of helplessness. A total freedom, they said, but that was rather repulsive to her. And there were those horrible shoes, sneakers or flat shoes that made women walk as ducks. Let alone the round-ended high heel shoes that to be more comfortable only made higher to belittle. No wonder desire was down. How a man could desire a woman in such attire? A sign of the times, that was not sufficiently studied, nonetheless a prefiguration. A long cycle that was not to be ended soon.

But all the videos were totally useless. None of these models, catwalking on her TV screen, was likely to be involved in the assassinations. She was looking for a man. Possibly, among those who stood backstage. But how could she know? Gabriella was, moreover, two or three years younger than she was and still active on the catwalk when she had already retired. She would have known other persons who were more challenging to identify. She could try to find her last shows or her last shootings in the magazines, but she would be losing her time. Nothing could make her sure that Gabriella had met the one she sought in the fashion world. She could instead have met him outside of it in the animal rights circles that she have been part of for fifteen years or so. It was more likely, even if her intuition told her it might not be so. And, if it was so, as she was contented with signing petitions but did not participate in demonstrations or any other actions, she had no trail and did not know what to do.

Another element came into play. The victims, two of them at least, had been chosen for their wives' proximity to Gabriella, but this very intention hid, indeed, another one. Why did they had the same physical type that had intrigued and disturbed her so much? Obviously, the choice of the targets did not only hinge on one criterion. As if a new selection had been made after a first choice. For she could not imagine that all the food processing industry leaders shared the same appearance. However, there was a coalescence between the logistics provided by her friend and the decisions others had taken.

There was this woman Gabriella told her about on the phone, who, maybe, monitored everything... From the center of Africa...

When Marc who had taken care of leaving her alone to conduct her research in the magazines, and on the videos, came into her office on Sunday evening, she admitted she was desperate to find a culprit to the three murders. He smiled, walked the room, lifted up a lock of his greyish hair falling onto his face and told her that they would finally find and when they would, perhaps they... He did not finish and suggested that they go out for a car ride.

Contrary to her changing clothes several times a day as nineteenth-century French treaties recommended to every woman who wanted to be elegant, she kept on her mid-thigh length greige-colored dress and only took off her gold-colored straps sandals to replace them with platform soles pumps, golden too, that would make her driving more complicated but... Maybe he would like to drive, but never, absolutely never, she could tolerate that someone else sat behind her Corvette's wheel.

His calm upset her and, as they drove to Siesta Key, the beach would be desert at this time of the evening, she wanted to ask him which part he was playing in this case. What would he want to do when they would have identified the culprit? But she changed her mind. Not that she was respecting the silence he might have wished to impose on them on their way to the beach, but she was pleased not knowing what he intended to do.

The last swimmers were leaving Siesta Beach, and they did not struggle to park in front of the sea. She took off her shoes, grabbed them in her hand and walked barefooted in the sand. It was still warm, and she feared she might get burned, but she soon reached the shore and walked in the water that was lapping in the setting sun. A postcard romantic photograph, she thought. Unbearable. Marc would agree. He had followed her but stayed some yards behind her on the beach. When she got out of the water and joined him, they walked side by side for a long time while he still was silent. Then, as dusk was falling, he stopped and asked in a voice she found eerie:

"Have you ever heard of the Quicksilver Surfer?"

"The comic book superhero?"

"Not the Silver Surfer. No. The Quicksilver guy".

22.

At the beginning of the afternoon, on the terrace of the big house that over-viewed the bay, Annelise, who was seated on an array of white cushions between Gabriella's thighs while she was massaging her shoulders, was waiting for her husband to be back. And it was the first time, indeed, she had been waiting for him with some impatience. She was itching for knowing how the meeting had been going...

If Gabriella, after admitting the precautions that David and Annelise wanted her to take were welcome, had approved them all, she had demanded that the latter's husband, while he was in Nairobi, did a last favor and performed what had been scheduled. Annelise did not know what this favor was about nor the details of what had been planned. Still, when he called, some days after Gabriella's arrival, she told him about the precautionary measures they all needed to take but reminded him as well that he could and even had to honor what was already planned. He would not go farther on, he assured. Then, as she insisted to know what it was all about, Gabriella had finally admitted that their organization, at least a branch of it, was taking new directions, bolder, more radical, and, as all revolutionary organizations, peaceful at first, it entered into armed struggle. She should know it better that everybody else, as a South African. Was not the African National Congress initially a nonviolent organization, founded on the exact model of Mahatma Gandhi's Indian National Congress? Then, facing the white Apartheid government's indifference to their struggle, had they not changed strategy, performed terror acts, and killed people? Nelson Mandela himself... And she could very well give other examples...

She also explained they had to exfil one of their fighters, one of their most valiant fighters, who arrived the day before in Kenya. As she knew that her husband was in the capital, she had asked him to provide logistical support: a car and money. At first, she did not want to tell her who was this brave fighter, but as she repeatedly insisted, she ended up telling her she knew him, almost a compatriot. Then, as Annelise had obviously guessed, she pronounced his name.

After all, she was not so much surprised. A logical follow-up, she had sensed. Even the name of their friend was utterly evident. They had often been together. She remembered the days they spent on the Malibu beaches where they watched him ride the waves on his surfboard, the nights in his Lauren Canyon's mansion where they were, three decades later, the other "Ladies of the Canyon", the yuppie version instead than the hippie one, who had been celebrated, at the end of the Sixties in a Joni Mitchell's song. Their talks, his commitment, and the intelligence of his arguments. Their collaboration before the camera, once, for a swimwear brand. His stunning beauty… His…

That her husband had met him disturbed her, and even excited her, sexually. And Gabriella's hands that slipped on her shoulders and sometimes reached up to the tender base of her neck…

She looked at the ocean, then her revolver she had put down on a coffee table with the butt shining in the sun. She did not know what she would be doing when he came back but she was waiting impatiently for his return. She thought of David too. Should he be kept posted? Would he have found that new lion cub Gabriella had asked for?

Gabriella suddenly stopped massaging her. The music is missing, she said. One of this Bossa Nova tune they were fond of, at night, in that L.A. mansion on the hill. She agreed and invited her to open the computer in the living room, made up her mind for the titles she liked on You Tube and to get connected to the Bluetooth speaker that was somewhere in the boudoir. Gabriella complied and disappeared into the shadows of the house. When she came back, a sweet and sensuous music was already filling the house, and reaching the terrace. She slowly swayed her hips to the rhythm of a sad samba, took off her printed dress despite the coolness and, in swimwear, came back to her.

She let her resume her massaging that little by little turned into caressing and asked if he would stay in Nairobi. No, she answered, he would leave soon and go where nobody could ever get him. Her answer was peremptory and did not authorize other questions. And she had no intention to ask her. She simply thought that one of the branches of their own organization or one of the AFL networks David told her about and he did not totally master the complexity of would take charge of him, in Africa or elsewhere.

When the first piece of samba was over and was followed by another one, less sad, more furious, with saxophone solos, she repelled Gabriella and told her she was cold. She suggested they went in the jacuzzi, but the other one declined.

The revolver was still shining on the table and she saw her back in the shooting range, where she took her some days before. As a beginner, she had been admired by the club's heads, reaching the target's heart with many of her bullets. She had watched her shoot in the battle dress pants she had traveled with and appropriately got in again, her hands together on the gun handle, with noise-cancelling headphones hiding part of her short blond hair. She had read in the concentration and aggressiveness she was demonstrating a sort of frustration. Something that talked about herself, too. Something that did worry her.

She entered into the jacuzzi, blew her hair straight back, and looked at the sky. She did not feel anymore her presence and, indeed, when she sat up, Gabriella was gone. She watched again the revolver still shining in the setting sun.

23.

Marc had called him the "Quicksilver guy", for by the end of last century, he had been quite successful on the West Coast posing for the tee-shirts of this brand specialized in surfing apparel. He had also posed at the time for the brand's swimwear collection in an advertising campaign Gabriella and Annelise were also part of. He was known for being very handsome. But he might even have been too handsome to become a celebrity. Even more since fashion photography had tried to question the classical canons of beauty. If, for women, they did resist, for men, as they never had really existed, to be too handsome was instead a handicap. Had he been a woman, yes, he would have reached a higher level of fame.

But, most of all, and it was what his sources taught him, some years later, he had become and still was the lover – the gigolo, some were saying – of this very well-known Eighties top-model, who became afterwards as well-known as an animal rights activist. And she had disappeared three months ago from all the media where she was very visible. Rumors had been circulating. Some said she was dead, other she was depressed, and further, simply, that she was making a movie. However, it seemed that it was the man they were looking for and perhaps his sponsor.

When, on Siesta Beach, he had given her the results of his phone calls, those calls she thought were not related to their case, Janice was sorry not to have found anything on her side. Even if she was not retired from modeling, she had not participated in the advertising campaign he mentioned. Still, rather that finding and enjoying images of her, she should have instead searched for Gabriella's. She might have seen, then, images of that man she ignored everything of so far. It was a time, actually, she was in New York or in Europe, in Italy mostly, and she had not run so much into Gabriella who had settled down for a while in California.

She asked him if he knew them both and if he had ever captured them in his objective. As to the former, no, he never had had the opportunity to break into man fashion, he even did not remember to have ever shot a male model, only soldiers but it was a long time before, in his prehistory! As to her, if they had roughly the same age, he came into the fashion photography world belatedly at the very end of the Eighties, when her modeling career was already over. But he remembered that he was proposed, quite recently, to make some sort of erotic movie with animals in which she had to appear.

She needed no images to know how the "mistress" looked, her face being known to everyone, the younger generations included. But this Monday, after a night that ended up in the first hours of the afternoon, she wanted to be showed a photograph of the "lover" or the "gigolo" no matter how he was called. He opened his computer, and after browsing on several sites, he turned the machine to her. The man who appeared on the screen in a Quicksilver tee-shirt was unknown to her; she was sure not to have ever met him in real life, nor in these places that already are anterooms of dream as a photography studio or the shooting set wherever it stood, but, instead, his virtual image was not totally unknown to her. It had likely been engraved on her retina while she was reading a magazine or looking at advertising. Marc was right: he was, indeed, perhaps too handsome.

Later, during the day, Marc had new phone conversations that came after one another till the evening. If he kept the name of the interlocutor secret, he did not forget to quickly inform her of what they had been talking about.

He taught her that checks had been carried out and it had proved possible to trace the one who had organized everything. She was not dead, nor depressed and, to his knowledge, was not making a movie. Still, she had left the United States for Africa, where at the heart of the continent, somewhere next to the sources of the Nile, in a troubled area, she had some kind of compound built that was destined to become the headquarters for her different operations. She had been living there for three weeks now, with her favorite animals and surrounded by local populations. For this, she certainly had benefited from support and complicity, from the government of the concerned countries to begin with but from some private donors, sympathizers of her struggle too. She had been seen in Cape Town and Johannesburg not that long ago.

He taught her too that she had a physical difference her fans had surely never heard of when she had so carefully applied herself to preserve from them over the decades – she was said to have set two of her dogs on those who had approached her. However, this difference was the following: she was deaf in one ear. Which one, nobody knew. It was possibly in a photo reportage in Africa, during her most significant years and the hunting party that followed, she experienced hearing loss in an accident.

Janice had carefully listened to him and did not know what to think, of him, of all that story. Were it not their own deductions that dragged them to such an improbable script? Their own fantasies, too? She came close to doubting the actual reality of the assassinations. Yet, on the other side, everything seemed to match so well: the murders, the sponsors, the executioners, and all that stood in between... She looked at Marc with his feet firmly planted in the middle of her wide living room. He seemed so sure of everything, of the story he had told, the interpretation he put forth, of himself. A slight smirk parted his lips:

"Is Gabriella still in Cape Town at Annelise's?"

"As far as I know, she is. She emailed me this morning".

"Didn't she tell you she met her once?"

"Yes, she did".

He walked away, stroked his hair back, seemed to do some thinking for some seconds, and took on a determined look:

"Then we have to fly to Cape Town. As soon as possible. Text Gabriella".

She was to protest but he did not let her the time to:

"You've never been to Africa before, have you? No better opportunity for you to get there. I'm sure you'll love it".

24.

Her husband came back late, later than it was planned. Either the flight from Nairobi had been delayed, or there were other reasons she did not try to find out. But then, she was no more excited. Because of the news, perhaps, Gabriella had come up with. When Gabriella had been back on the terrace, as she was getting out of the Jacuzzi, she told that she had just received a message from Janice saying that Marc and she would come to Cape Town in the following days. She did not know Marc and had only crossed Janice on the catwalk, but the announcement of their arrival introduced something new, something more dramatic... Because of her yoga exercises too, she was doing everyday at nightfall, that kept her concentrated on her body and made her forget all the rest in the contemplation of the starry sky. Anyhow, when her husband came at last and found the two of them lying half naked on a bed, she did not find anything else to say but "Have a good night's sleep". He hesitated, greeted Gabriella, and then went up the stairs where, a moment later, a boy followed him carrying his vast suitcase.

Gabriella would have wished to know if everything had been going all right in Nairobi and she blamed her for having dismissed him too quickly. Annelise hissed between her teeth, saying that she did not care anymore and that, by no means, she could stand to see him. And she invited her to go to sleep, too.

It was only the following day, as Annelise was still sleeping and she was having breakfast with her husband who woke up early, she could make sure he had done what had been planned. As she had wished, her valiant fighter had taken possession of an all-terrain vehicle and a substantial amount of money in several local currencies. Nevertheless, he told her that if he could more or less guess what it was all about, he did not want to know, and, from now on, he only wanted to consider simple transactions for animal conservation, and the fight against poaching. It was necessary for the smooth running of his own businesses since, in several of their British networks, they were somehow linked to food processing industries and even if he tried to respect as far as it was possible the animal welfare, contrary to his French and American colleagues, he did not want and could not oppose them. It was an important matter for his marriage, too...

When he left for a meeting in the Cape Town Parliament, the inaugural speech would begin, as always, said he, with "All protocols observed", Gabriella wondered what he had meant. Their political positioning was perhaps the only thing they had in common and the only domain in which they could find some matter of agreement, Annelise having never been an activist, rather a sympathizer of the animal rights. Otherwise... How, beyond strictly financial interests this couple could remain together? Annelise's previous marriages had rapidly dissolved. And between them they were casual lovers and a permanent one. And there was herself... At least she wished it, even if... She remembered that he had been for a while on the list of the would-be victims, but that he was finally taken out for pragmatist reasons as well as for other, more ideological, reasons.

Annelise came down at last and when she appeared never had she seen her as pretty.

Even not in their California time, when... She was dressed in her riding attire and had splendidly made up. Not that conspicuous makeup that enlarged the eyes and turned the face into an expressionless mask, but a light makeup that, even with several layers, conveyed an impression of freshness and of sensuousness as extreme as improbable. An ideal figure in the most down-to-earth reality.

She saw her take a bottle of ice-tea out of the fridge and drink a glass of it, then to rub her lips with a light red lipstick. She did not speak, only watched her. And she did not found in her friend that excitement that caught her up the previous day when she was waiting for her husband, nor the indifference that was a substitute for it in the night, when he came back home late. Now, she was only serene and determined.

"I'm going for a ride on the beach", she said, before taking her revolver and slipping it under the belt of her riding pants.

From a window, she watched her, below, talk to the black groom and disappeared in the stables. And she pictured her riding on the beach, caressing her horse's neck, the sand blowing under the hooves. She had never wished to go riding with her, not having this love of horses that was hers. Just as for men, she noticed. As she left her vantage point, came back to her mind these words she heard once, she did not remember who had pronounced them, possibly another model, nor the circumstances. Terrible words: "My mouth filled up with sperm". And that, she was now convinced, had made her dislike forever men... she had never liked. She thought of her cats, on the other side of the ocean, of her new lion cub she had soon to get. She saw her again taking her gun and slipping it under her belt and pictured her days earlier, at the shooting range. Then she rushed in her bedroom, took off her clothes, and lay naked on the purple blanket of the bed that just had been made. And she looked at the ceiling, so white, so glassy where she was sure she saw the reflection of her body, entirely painted in green, ochre and black motives.

25.

Marc was driving the car, a Chevrolet the model he did not care of, they had rented in Sarasota and they would leave at Miami International airport. A night flight to Sao Paulo, then another night flight the next day to South Africa, with a more critical jet lag to get over, but they were both used to it.

They had been driving along the West Coast for a while and, in Naples, they had turned off eastwards on Alligator Alley and, on this road, she always revived her memory. When she was a child, she had the surprise, and the delight, to see an alligator crossing the freeway before her parents' Cadillac. Sharp braking and a swerve and they were heading to the ditch, and she only had time to see the reptile composedly sliding into the Everglades. The Everglades, that land and real estate speculation would destroy before long. She had joined the Everglades Forever Act, some time ago, and was teaming with Seminoles Indians, rather black than red, who affectionately called her "sister".

After the intersection with the Florida Turnpike, they left the Interstate 75 and drove along the coast between Port Everglade and Miami. Passing Fort Lauderdale-Hollywood airport, she reminded him that, on a perfectly blue sky December day in 1945, from this airport, a naval air base at the time, had taken off Flight 19, these five US Navy Avengers which was born the Bermuda Triangle's legend from. He nodded, he knew, and smiled when she confessed that, she had already been living in Florida for some time; as she came from Palm Beach and stopped, another December day by the beach side, under a gray and threatening sky, she saw a strange jet taking off, skimming over the waves and disappearing in the clouds at the horizon... She also thought that there, off Fort Lauderdale, as she had read it lately, was written a song the lyrics spoke of a departure, on wooden ships, to somewhere it would be possible to laugh out again, likely after a nuclear cataclysm or an ecological disaster. But she did not share her thoughts with Marc who brought her back to reality. He told her he wondered why Gabriella was staying in Cape Town for such a long time. What did she come for? What was she preparing? Whom did she get her orders from? Would she go elsewhere in Africa? She would have to answer all those questions unless she did not want to see them and was already gone when they would come. She suggested that she might simply be a woman in love. In love with Annelise. He looked at her. He was aware of Gabriella's gender preferences, while he had no idea what were Annelise's, but... Remained the question of her connection to the one who now lived in the heart of Africa.

"She only met her once, didn't she?"

"Indeed, that's what she said on the phone".

Once, only once. Not much, but it was preferable that they never saw each other or at least no more than needed and only communicated with no physical presence. It was, indeed, the world we were entering. Inevitably. A world in which physical contact was minimized and was no more the prime vector of communication. The world of the younger generations, not his, perhaps already Gabriella's and Janice's world... And if they only met once, where did they meet? In Cape Town may be, as Gabriella was a frequent visitor to the city. But it did not matter much… No, it did not matter at all.

In Hollywood Beach, they had to stop to a red light, as a bridge drew up to let a boat sail past on the Waterway. Those terrible Floridian bridges to which the cars have to wait while the boats go on. Hundreds of vehicles for only one boat. The passengers of the vehicles around grinned and bore it, without realizing the situation's absurdity. They did know it even if they were not in a hurry and with no consulting they applauded when the bridge went down and they could keep up going as the boat pursued his ghostly sailing in the middle of the lands.

They passed Hallande and, always on the oceanside soon reached where Ocean Drive became Collins Avenue and Miami Beach separated from Miami. They had left hastily, with a minimum luggage, and Janice intended to complete her initial equipment with an hour or two of shopping spree in Bal Harbor, as in compensation to the anguish that was gripping on her. Then, the Julia Tuttle Bridge would take them to the airport. So, farther on, when they began to see Downtown Miami skyscrapers, they pulled over next to

Bal Harbor's *Plaza* and, forgetting the heat, they paced the streets and boutiques up and down.

She did not consider the bags and shoe shops she was used to – she had what she needed – and renounced to enter Ralph Lauren. She was tempted by Stella McCartney, her fluid dresses, and suits. Still, despite the designer's vegan stance she tried several pants at Loro Piana's, bought one and finally found most of what she was looking for at Dior's and Balenciaga's. She hesitated between a sequined mini-dress and a camisole at La Perla's, but the former was not appropriate to where she was going, and she made her mind up for the latter. The bras at Agent Provocateur's drew her attention for a while, but she never wore one and had never understood why women, at least the small breasted ones kept on wearing it or began again. She regarded it as a regression of feminism, and sexual liberation as well. Marc had followed her in her shopping spree, taking pleasure on going back in the time when, if he did not dress her, he photographed her, clothed or naked. He regretted not having his camera with him. When she was finished, she complained about La Martina not having a shop in Bal Harbor. He could have found polo outfits well adapted to their African expedition. She suggested they tried Vilebrequin instead. He did not refuse, let her drag him into the shop and after he bought at the St Tropez brand linen multi pocketed pants, he admitted they were appropriate. Even more if they had to go and get her where she was, at heart of Africa.

26.

He had emptied out his mag, first shooting at a road sign then randomly in the wilderness. The sun was beating down every bit as firmly in the Rift Valley and the altitude made it difficult to breathe. He caught his breath and put his pistol back into the glove box of the car. There was no one around and the shots were still ringing in his ears.

His shirt was dirty, but he had not wished to substitute for it the white shirt and navy-blue Nehru-collar tunic he had bought from a Nairobi Indian shop. He only had swapped his chinos for battle dress pants, his only other slacks, in the large pockets of he had shoved rolls of banknotes. The night was falling. He had left late, and the border was still far away. He did not know yet if he would look after one of those rarer lodges as he drove northwestwards or if he would sleep in the Range Rover. The immensity of the landscape was inviting, but it had not this protective aspect he found in the American West.

It was on one of these roads that he had first met her, ten years ago. She was riding a Harley Davidson somewhere in the Mojave desert. She pivoted slowly and, driving his Sixties Dune Buggy Meyers Manx, he passed her, only keeping in mind the fugitive image of a blond, almost white hair blowing in the wind and a mature woman's weathered face. He met her up in Barstow, in a demonstration for the environment he and other AFL members were taking part of.

He had been told who she was. And knowing what she had represented for a previous generation and the star she still was in the movies, he did not dare get close to her. But if she was cold and distant, even arrogant when she spoke with a French or sometimes Germanic accent that tinted her English, their past career in fashion had rapidly made them closer. As, later, common African origins, for she was born from French and German parents, in Morocco, close to that Algeria the tragedy had played a significant role in the Rhodesian UDI. "White male colonist" she labeled him once.

For all that concerned animal rights and to a lesser degree nature conservation, she was fanatical. She was in all demonstrations from the North Pole to the most far flung lands in Africa and Asia, before the American slaughterhouses to the United Nations; she created foundations; spoke out in the media, everywhere she could be heard and expected to be heard. Compared to her he was such a neophyte that even his more significant commitment could not impress her. Her gigolo too, some long lasting stories were saying. She was fifteen years older than he... Yet... Other stories said she was a man who, still young, had undergone surgery before she became a very well-known model and a photographic icon. Her height maybe, six foot tall, almost as high as he was... But if she was not far from grounding them once when she asked him, one night, how he felt to sleep with a woman who was actually a man, he had never tried to check by himself – how could he have? – preferring to keep her initial sex uncertain.

Did he kill these men because he loved her? No. He did not believe it. Instead his own convictions, his convictions for a cause that had to get more dramatic, more symbolic, more disturbing actions to have its audience enlarged and to be under the new world it aimed at creating. He felt like retrieving his pistol, shooting again, hearing in the harsh loneliness of the bush the bang of the shots. But he decided to move on and to sleep in that loneliness. He would cross the border the next day, drive through Uganda, Mbale, Gulu, dirt roads and other boundaries and enter this territory she was the queen of, at heart of Africa. She would be her guide when he would contact her through the radio.

When, before he set off, he fixed the rear-view mirror in a mechanical reflex, he found himself in front of an impassive and serene, vaguely smiling, face, as in a Buddha statue. He felt no tension in him, only a void as, once, when standing on his surfboard he rode the long ocean waves, in Zuma Beach. The ocean was far away, even farther away than from the place he was born in. Between the profound continent and its shores, he had never made up his mind. Now he had. He was going back in the quietness of the savannas and the forests.

He went in the African dusk, heard the rustle of the air beyond his half-opened windows, the screams, perhaps, of the wild animals. He drove for a long time, slowly, his eyes on a road that, in the end, did not exist anymore. He thought he saw in the headlights he had just switched on, forms of felines on the side of the road, then, after a village, on a dirt road leading in the depth of the bush he finally stopped. He lay down on his seat, switched the engine and the lights of the car off, and he closed his eyes, confronting his own darkness the darkness of the surrounding nature.

The nothingness firstly, then her own face, hieratic, with transparent eyes surrounded with blonde, almost white, hair, which soon was substituted for a lion's face, or rather a lioness' but with a mane. These three dark eyed men he shot she had selected with Gabriella's help. Very carefully. In the name of the race. As animals were sorted out on race criteria and was decided on beauty criteria which would be preserved, she sorted out men on race criteria and decided on ugliness criteria who would be executed.

27.

Gabriella and Annelise came to meet them at the Camps Bay POD where they had settled down and where they were next two teams of photographers and models making advertising films for the South African television. And when, in this late afternoon, they appeared in the hotel hall where Marc was waiting for them, they had attracted their attention. Annelise was still very well-known in her country and, to many of the current models was someone to follow and imitate. So, when Janice, in turn, came down, Marc had not been able to reach them yet.

After chatting for some long minutes, they managed to escape their admirers' group and came to meet them. Janice took pleasure to see Gabriella again and Marc was fascinated by Annelise's beauty he judged intact even if he had only known her through the magazine photographs. A turquoise necklace increased it even more. And her strappy little cocktail black dress that undressed her more than it dressed her... He should have, fifteen years earlier, integrated her in her nude photographs... with Janice and Gabriella. But would she have complied? It might not be too late...

They went and sat in a hotel salon overlooking the pool and the ocean. Janice was tempted to talk to Annelise in Dutch but, had her answered in Afrikaans, she might not have understood. And she did not want to add an odd language to an already odd situation. Annelise had put on her shoulders a white jacket and, watching Marc, crossed and uncrossed her legs while Gabriella stayed stone-faced in her sand-colored jumpsuit. But they only arrived in the morning, with the same tiresome flights Gabriella had been flying on ten days earlier. It might be their tiredness that made her feel everything was strange, or, even more simply, her first contact with a country she did not know but which coastline had something that could remind her of the Californian coast she had grown up on. Finally, Marc started to speak and said he had not been back in South Africa for almost twenty-two years, when he had covered as a young photo-reporter, Nelson Mandela's release from his residential surveillance in Paarl. It was before he began his career in fashion, far before he met two of them and they posed naked in that photograph that had been seen all around the world. He looked at Annelise in turn, insistently, as to show he was sorry she had not been in it. He would have created a part for her, as he had invented in the morning, these flames that surfaced again at the rear of the cabin, when their plane descended to the Oliver Tambo airport in Johannesburg. He chased away the images that came back to him, *Just my imagination*, and suggested they went up in his room.

Under a bellboy's indifferent gaze, they walked a corridor, and he introduced them to the large suite he shared with Janice. He closed the curtains on the sun beginning to go down upon the horizon into the ocean and switched on a lamp in the living room. He went to the mini bar and asked what they wanted to drink, but all three declined.

"She never killed anybody", Gabriella told him when he asked her what her relations to that woman living at the heart of Africa were. Sure, she had never killed anybody, but she sent her boys to do the job, likewise Charlie Manson, who had not killed anybody but sent Susan Atkins and some others to slaughter Sharon Tate and her friends in her Benedict Canyon's house during the 1969 summer. She would have adhered to his recent ATWA doctrine, might have already adhered. And she could even have attached to Helter Skelter at that time. After he had made this point, Gabriella who obviously did not know what he was referring to, did not find anything to answer. But when he asked her if she knew where *he was*, after a moment of hesitation she shook her head to mean that, yes, she knew. She hesitated, then told him that Annelise's husband had met him, some days ago, in Nairobi, Kenya and had provided him with everything that he would need to join her. If he had not faced unexpected obstacles, he would be now with her or, in any case, was on his way to get to her.

Janice who was wearing one of the blue woolen pants suits she had bought in Bal Harbor at Balenciaga was watching them from the sofa she was seated on, a leg folded under the other. She had not intervened, contented with listening. Now she could read in Gabriella's eyes a total self-assurance that Marc had not shaken off and she had seen a slight sneer on Annelise's face when was mentioned her husband's meeting with the Quicksilver surfer. The two women seemed united in a shared silence that could very well be a secret.

There was a time during which one they were all in front of themselves, to the exception of Annelise who, straight in her armchair, crossed legged, kept on watching Marc, amazed. Janice put an end to it, asking Marc:

"What are you gonna do next?"

At first, he did not answer, frowned, and looked at each one to gauge them. Then he said they were going to get her where she was. They knew where. They would rent a plane. And he wished Gabriella and Annelise to come on with them.

28.

When he woke up, it had not dawned yet. Everything was quiet around him. No bird calls, no cries of wild animals. Only the silence. The silence of the bush, the Rhodesian bush he was born in...

He took the water bottle next to his pistol out of the glove box, opened it, and drank a mouthful. He was for eating some corn grains he had rolled up in a chapatti, but he decided to fast, as he often was doing when he was a model. He groped for his briefcase and bag, and the additional spare wheel on the backseat, then put the key in the ignition, switched on the lights and hit the road again.

Soon, between the mountains in the east the dawn was breaking, and he drove faster than he had done the day before. He knew there would be a lot of trucks at the Uganda border, on the Malaba River, he would waste time, would have to give money, and he wished he could get there before the sun went high in the sky.

He had to be patient, indeed, and he waited behind a queue of trucks. When it was his turn, to avoid waiting again and a possible custom's examination, he took out of his pocket a roll of banknotes. He slid it in his passport, on which the custom officer was soon stamping a one-month visitor's visa. Then, a barrier was lifted, and the road opened again before him.

The road was large and despite some trucks, bikes or groups of children on roadsides that slowed him somehow, he could drive fast. He did not take time to admire the landscape of a country that Churchill had once described as the pearl of Africa, he ate up the miles, avoiding towns and villages and only stopping, in open spaces, to satisfy his more elementary physiological needs, and he reached Gulu at the beginning of the afternoon.

In the only restaurant he judged possible to eat something, and where several waiters were crowding around him, he looked at the road map of the region. He would need three hours, may be more, to reach Arua, the last town before the borders, where the savannas turned into the equatorial forests and the road might be more arduous, invaded by laterite and potholes, and where he knew he had to spend the night.

When he crossed the metal bridge over the Nile Albert past Pakwach, he thought again of her, what he has not done, he only realized then, since the previous day. Their life together. His life without her, his life with her. He thought again of their very first meeting. Her Harley Davidson and he did not like the motorbikes! Nor did she, now... no more than the cars. She was elegant, and determined, and arrogant too when she pleaded her cases. And exigent... Her terrible exigencies... She did not like men but animals. Life had made her hate the former and love the latter. Boredom most of all... When he went along some hills, one of them, with her nipple-like form reminded him the description of a landscape in this African adventures' novel that sent him back to his own history. Saba's breast... Once, he was playing with the tips of her breasts and was wondering how firm they were, as she had always claimed she had never resorted to plastic surgery, he made the connection. The breast of a Saba doomed to be immortal, he told her. But he was mistaking. She would not be eternal. And that was why he was going to meet her.

Before he could meet her, there was still a long road ahead. Borders again when they had dreamed and always dreamed of having them abolished. City and village names, Aru, Faradje and Aba to the north. And a troubled area where transited the Uganda's Tutsi on their way to Rwanda and where those fleeing the new South Sudan sought refuge, in the reverse route, their own ancestors might have followed when they were going down the Nile... The North-Eastern Congo's gold mines, as if they were King Solomon's ones. As in California too, once, Fort Sutter and the Swiss general's first gold deposit. And animals, monkeys he knew she would be surrounded with... She had settled down the edges of the worse place in the world but, it might be, the best one too. The Mekong's muddy delta and the Shangri-la's green pastures at a same area...

The landscape was changing, plains with lush vegetation were taking over the hills. The road was getting bad and, in the end, there was no road at all. It took him a long time, at least it was what he thought, to get to Arua. The night was falling and after hesitating and going in the wrong direction, he stopped in the only hotel that looked like a hotel.

The next day he would go on. He would switch the radio on, she would be her guide and he would enter her kingdom where time would not exist anymore.

29.

David Vargas had had an exhausting day in the reserve and, before going to bed, he had not taken time to watch the evening news as he was used to. So, when he woke up, on Tuesday morning, his first reflex, before his breakfast, was to switch the television on. He did not care much of the "Breaking News" that were scrolling at the bottom of the screen in a South African news program and were announcing what seemed to be a plane crash and even less of the quick mention, at the end of the program, of a Western Cape businessman's gun death. Businessmen as ordinary people's murders in South Africa were not rare but happened everyday so that they were so ordinary matter they were not paid the attention they should have been paid. If plane crashes were more occasional, they did not stir up in him this unhealthy curiosity that they did in other persons, may be because of the dramatic number of people they implied…

Thus, he forgot the short news item, had breakfast, and got ready for the day. The television was still on, but before switching it off and leaving the bungalow, almost for fun, he went to another network, still another one, till he reached CNN. To his own surprise the American news network was speaking of the accident and was giving more details that he had read on the Breaking News banner. In fact, it was not an accident or not one yet but a plane that had not been heard of and that had disappeared from the radar screens the night before somewhere over Africa. The aircraft was a business jet, a Learjet 70, that had taken off from Cape Town International to Libreville at the beginning of the afternoon. It had stopped over at Luanda and it was, an hour or so after it took off from the Angola capital, that all the communications were lost. There was no reason to consider right now that the aircraft had crashed. No distress signal had been sent and no ground impact had been reported in the zones the plane was to fly over.

He smiled. Another of these African stories, as in the recent past. Everybody had remembered this plane that disappeared from Luanda airport, precisely, nine years ago almost to the day. A Boeing 727 that had been pinned to the ground for fourteen months in default of payment had been seen by the control tower as it was moving on the runways. The plane had been taking off with no authorization to an unknown destination. It was never found after intensive search had been carried on all over Africa by the United States who feared the aircraft might be used to terrorist purpose. Another robbery, obviously, and the Learjet 70 that was a smaller plane and could land on dirt runways would be even harder to locate. Nevertheless, he opened his computer, in the hope of finding additional details on the CNN site. He did not find anything more than what had been said on the television but that the Learjet and his pilot had been rented on Sunday by an American couple.

He did not know why, but this last point prevented him from going out and he stayed before his television set for new developments. He had not to wait for long, as the disappearance of the plane seemed to catch the attention of the media to channel energies and to raise hypotheses. If a technical failure or bad weather conditions – the weather was fine – could not be put forward, a robbery was, indeed, envisaged as a hijacking or an explosion on board provoked by a missile.

The last two explanations were pure speculation without grounding. A hijacking would have been claimed for and the plane would have been landing somewhere for a long time: the Learjet had a cruising range of four hours that is a little more than 2500 miles... As to a missile, on the one hand, from where and by whom could it had been shot on the plane route, on the other hand the explosion would have been heard on the radars. Moreover, the TV presenters were refuting them as soon as formulated and as far as he was concerned, he did not give them any credence... In compensation he had to admit that the plane rented with his pilot by this American couple, even if no more was known did question the robbery hypothesis... Remained the facts. The plane had not sent any signal after taking off from Luanda, either it had turned off the communication system to become invisible or it had really become invisible...

The flux of images and words that bustled on the screen as he went from one network to another overwhelmed him and bored him at last. And he was back on the South African network that did not speak of the lost plane. After a very short reportage, in Afrikaans, he did not understand, in a Cape Town suburb, a new reportage began with images of a beautiful residence close to Fish Hoek. He thought it might be Annelise's house where he had been several times. He turned it up. One was speaking, in English this time, of this businessman who had been found dead in his bathroom, the previous night, a bullet in the neck. His wife and a friend of her who had been staying in the house for some time were travelling. It was the guard who had discovered the corpse after his boss' company in Cape Town had been worried when he did not come into his office in the afternoon to sign some documents as he used to do. The heinous crime trail was privileged he heard, as he watched on the television two police cars parked before the property entrance.

He took his phone, called Annelise, but there were no ringing and no voice mail... A heinous crime... A bullet in the neck and a naked corpse in the bathtub. It was hard to believe. But he had no time to think of it anymore since another news flash interrupted the reportage. The anchor took stock of the circumstances of the Learjet disappearance and then announced that the passengers had been identified. And while she spoke, the names were encrusted on the screen:

- *Marc Fremont, US citizen, born 1957 in New York.*
- *Janice Dillon, US citizen, born 1975 in Sacramento.*
- *Gabriella Dicker, Brazilian citizen, born 1977 in Porto Alegre.*
- *Annelise de Jager, South African citizen, born 1977 in Cape Town.*

The presenter added that these four passengers were very well known. The first one was an ex war correspondent turned fashion photographer and the three other models whose faces had been on the magazine covers in their time. Two of them had posed, naked, for animal rights in his photographs that were worldwide famous and the last one was much appreciated in South Africa for her commitment to the animals. They still had been seen in a Camps Bay hotel on Saturday. She also said that the pilot was a Belgian citizen from Rwanda and had a respectful number of flying hours.

This last announcement stunned him, and now he understood why, when he had learned that the Learjet had been booked by an American couple, he had sensed... This American couple Annelise had told they were coming in their last phone call, on Friday if he remembered well, and assured they had not to be afraid of. She had not told who they really were, but, it seemed to him, that they were coming from Boca Raton, Florida, he knew well for the polo games he had been playing there, and that she took care of everything. She would call him later, when they would be there. These were her last words. But why had they all left? To go where? Where were they now? Why did she join them? And Gabriella?

He switched off his television set, still stunned. He would have to travel to Cape Town, before... Then he thought of the pilot. A Belgian citizen from Rwanda. He had known one, more precisely a Tutsi, he had been flying with some years ago. A bizarre fellow who believed in the Hereafter life, in aliens, and in lost paradises... But an excellent pilot who could land on any runways... He remained prostrated for a long moment, then he returned to his computer, looked for additional news. There was her husband's murder too. The press did not make any connection between the murder and the two women's travel. But when they left Cape Town, he might already have died. What happened? Was everything planned? The revolver Annelise was always carrying with her. Gabriella?

He did not find anything, but after long minutes during which he was watching the news as they came, always the same ones, on the circumstances of the plane disappearance, on the hypotheses that could explain it away, now on the passengers, too, he read that some minutes before descending to Luanda there was a last radio communication by the pilot, immediately followed, in the seconds before it was interrupted, by what sounded like sighs, of pleasure, coming from the cabin…

There was a knock on the bungalow door. He would have liked not to be disturbed. He hesitated and finally opened the door. A Reserve attendant told him that there would be soon two to four beautiful lion cubs birth.

www.ingramcontent.com/pod-product-compliance
Lightning Source LLC
LaVergne TN
LVHW031606060526
838201LV00063B/4751